Reflections
of
Rockingham

Rockingham Writers Centre

Anthology 2025

A catalogue record for this book is available from the National Library of Australia

ROCKINGHAM
WRITERS
CENTRE

ISBN-13: 978-0-6482016-7-0

Rockingham Writers Centre
11 Kent Street
Rockingham, Western Australia
https://rockinghamwriterscentre.org.au

An initiative of

FRIENDS OF ROCKINGHAM ARTS COMMUNITY

Dedication

This book is dedicated to the pioneers of Rockingham who paved the way to put Rockingham on the map, to the town planners and residents who continue to contribute to its growth and to those in the future who will keep the city a place of pleasure, beauty and prosperity.

Contents

A Dog's Breakfast

D. Alan Petersen

'Don't look now, but your boyfriend's back!' whispered Serena.

Bree refused to rise to the bait, instead funnelled her annoyance into the noisy task of churning out the cappuccino.

An amused exhalation was Serena's parting shot, before dashing off with the tray for table thirteen.

Glancing up, Bree watched Serena sashaying through the Saturday morning hubbub. She moved more like a supermodel on a Paris catwalk than a waitress serving coffees at Rockingham Beach's Dôme. Shoulders slumping, Bree slid the cappuccino onto a tray and started the next. It was bad enough that Serena was a stunner; worse was her uncanny ability to read people, and their minds, it seemed, hers in particular. *Damn her!*

Giving up on Serena, she turned her gloom onto what *she* was going to do about Saturday morning's perpetual first customer, or any other interesting man for that matter. The trouble was, right now, she just didn't have time for anything but Uni and work. It was a right now that apparently had no end. Another wistful sigh was released into the noise and steam above the espresso machine before she refocused on the question of why he was back. He'd never done that before.

Raising her head, Bree let her eyes brush over the queue. There he stood, second from the end, tall, trim and resplendent in a pale-pink linen shirt with sandy-coloured pleated trousers. She couldn't resist lingering, for a microsecond, on his face and again felt the glow of its strength, vitality, compassion and … hints of nervousness around the piercing blue eyes? She'd never seen that before. How very odd. It was another mystery sent to bedevil her.

Her speculation was cut short by Cathy's hurried passing over of the next drinks order before racing back to her spot at the till. Skewering the order on the spike, Bree grabbed a cup and submerged her increasingly jumbled emotions by chiselling away at the growing backlog of orders, her mood improving with each cathartic bashing out of the spent coffee grounds.

During the fifteen-minute avalanche that followed, Bree kept one eye on "her" man's progress, saw him shuffle forward whilst taking a call on his mobile, and later noted his more relaxed posture. At the next glance, he was second in line. Her last view was of his departure, *outside*. She almost overcooked the flat white from the shock. He *never* went outside!

Images returned of that morning, eight months ago – on their first day back after being closed for a month for renovations – to find him at the door, bang on seven-thirty. She was bringing out the first stack of chairs, which he had gallantly given her a hand with. He'd then explained that he arrived early to get a good spot *inside*. Her questioning frown had elicited his reason – he wasn't partial to being sniffed at by wandering dogs.

Serena, now working the till, broke into her reminiscing. 'It's a cappuccino for your man *and* a soy latté. He's also ordered brioche, fruit and poached eggs, for *two*!' she said with a toothy grin whilst waving the order around as if it were a winning Lotto ticket.

'Who's this man Serena's talking about?' asked Cathy, standing behind, waiting for her turn at making the coffees.

'He's *not* "my man", he's just a customer I like.'

With pursed lips and downcast eyes, Bree finished the cup she was brewing, then quickly squeezed past, grabbed the tray for table eighteen and escaped into the crowded room.

She delivered the next three orders without incident, each time giving her colleagues the silent treatment. Coming back for the fourth, she found both waiting, eyes gleaming, sporting knowing smiles as they guarded a tray bulging with plates and steaming cups.

'He's under the awning at the very end. Don't spill anything. And when you get back, we'll want a full report,' winked Serena, sliding the tray over.

It took all her willpower for Bree not to glare or drop the tray, then, without comment, she turned and carefully threaded her way towards the front doors. Beneath the calm, she was seething. The girls were being ridiculous. *She* was being ridiculous!

Outside, the cool, sea air and sunshine steadied her for a millisecond, until she turned right, and stopped. There he sat, ensconced with a glitzy brunette in a low-cut, red dress that left little to the imagination. Bloody hell, what was he doing with a floozy like that! How could she have got him so wrong? Straightening up, she took a breath and then walked over with as much dignity as she could muster.

'Your order, sir, madame.'

She spoke with stilted formality and immediately felt like a pompous idiot. Then remained standing, stiffly, for an overlong moment, waiting for who knew what.

'Thanks, Bree. Everything looks perfect, as usual. Thanks.'

The warmth in his smile and words revived her so much that she brushed aside the fierce disdain radiating from the woman, who was definitely mutton dressed as lamb.

'I hope you enjoy your meal,' she replied, again with undue formality.

Turning to go, she suddenly found herself blocked by a golden retriever looking up with enquiring eyes. It was one of a pair on extremely long leads, attached to a huffing and puffing, rotund, grey-haired lady in black leggings and a Bali T-shirt.

'Don't worry; they're friendly!'

Too friendly.

Bree suddenly found a wet doggie nose invading her crotch just as the other one arrived to slobber over the knees of her man's painted companion.

'Argh!' squeaked Bree, jerking backwards and falling onto the table behind.

'Argh!' cried the old gent at the table, mouth agape as he saw the croissant he was reaching for catapult into the air along with his untouched coffee.

'Argh! Go away, you brute!' yelled the woman in red.

Bree, now prostrate at the old guy's feet, continued to ward off the attentions of the first dog as the second received the flying coffee full force. It yelped and jumped onto the floozy in red, tipping her backwards past the point of no return.

She had time for one last 'Argh!' before, with legs flailing, she bumped her head on the pavement to lie stupefied with the slobbering, wriggling dog on top of her.

Bree's man had jumped up reflexively in a failed attempt to save his companion and, in doing so, upended their table, which launched more food and drink, this time towards Bree's amorous pooch. It was quick-witted enough to avoid the coffees and then as quick in making a start on gulping down the food so unexpectedly offered.

The second dog abandoned the woman in red to join in the messy feeding frenzy, its wagging tail fanning the fluttering eyes of the stunned temptress.

Eventually, the dogs' owner arrived, reined in both whilst offering profuse apologies for their unruly behaviour.

Bree's man phoned for an ambulance after telling his groggy companion to stay put until the ambos arrived, after which he helped Bree to her feet and, with her, and others, restored order.

Once the ambulance departed, Bree's man accompanied her back inside.

'What a disaster. What a dog's breakfast. I hope you'll be okay. You've had quite a shock,' he said with some emotion, before extracting a business card from his shirt pocket. 'If there are any complications, please give me a call, I may be able to help.'

Curiosity had Bree stopping to glance at the details. After all these months, she still didn't know his name. The card read: *Mr Alain Bergus, Hortense and Bergus Consulting Architects and Interior Designers.*

The name seemed vaguely familiar. To give her mind time to puzzle out why, she asked: 'What about your lady friend?'

'Mrs Vanstein? She's a client and will be okay. She's a tough one. So tough, I wouldn't put it past her to consider legal action. But that's nothing for you to worry about. I'll sort it out. If it happens.'

They continued inside, then halted at the counter.

An awkwardness developed.

Bree fingered the business card, then looked up to find Mr Bergus gazing down with an almost boyish expression that instantly fled when Serena barged in on them.

'Hello, Mr Bergus. Hope you survived the drama unscathed.'

'All under control now, thanks, Serena,' he said with a courteous nod.

She nodded back and then moved off to deliver her tray of drinks and snacks.

'You … errr … know Serena?' stammered Bree.

Mr Bergus chuckled.

'Y-e-s,' he stretched the word, 'Serena's a wonderful girl, but way too much for me. Perhaps …'

The raised eyebrows and expectant look had Bree's heart fluttering. Suddenly, she couldn't swallow.

He continued, 'Perhaps you'd like to have lunch with me sometime. Not here, of course.'

'Of course. Yes. I'll … errr … send you a text. Bye.' Bree turned, controlling her urge to run, and made it to the kitchen, then collapsed breathless onto a chair, woozy with delight.

Maybe Serena was right.

Maybe he is *my* man!

A Dog's Day

Dianne Johnson

A gentle breeze tosses my hair. I pick up pace, trying to keep up with Dexter as he pulls on his leash, always anxious to get on with his daily walk. Once a week, I take him to the local dog park. Today is the day.

We reach the fork in the pathway. Dexter looks one way then the other. He waits for my signal.

'Yes, Dexter, it's dog park day.'

His marble eyes shine with excitement as we walk sedately across the road. Safely on the footpath, I relax the leash and let him set the pace. Around the corner we jog, down the lane, past Buckly's mulberry tree, branches hanging tantalisingly over the fence, laden with ripe fruit. On we go, undistracted, straight to the Bayview Reserve Dog Park.

Looks like most of the gang are here already; there's Scout and Hunter, Benji, Shadow, Buster and little Cherry chihuahua. I unlatch the gate and sigh. 'Hi, guys, sorry we're a bit late today. Never mind, looks like you're all having fun.'

Freed from his leash, Dexter bounds towards the drainpipe tunnel and darts through, yapping with glee.

Shadow follows.

Next, he scurries over the wooden bridge, around the fallen log and then, rolling onto his back, legs in the air, enjoys a sand bath.

Barry laughs. 'Your Dexter really is the gang leader; look how all the others follow him.'

'Yes,' Connie agrees. 'You should have seen how quiet the others were before you two arrived. The dogs just walked around, nose to the ground, sniffing here and sniffing there, putting a little mark here and making their mark there. They really missed Dexter.'

I twirl the leash in my hand and smile. 'Oh, Dexter … he just loves coming here. How often do you bring Benji?'

'He'd come every day if he could, but we only come twice a week.'

'Yeah, same here, but I can only make it on a Wednesday when I'm on late shift.'

'Hoy! Buster,' Clive yells as he rescues the miniature chihuahua. 'None of that here, boy.'

'Oh, my baby,' cries Cassandra, clutching the tiny dog to her chest.

'You should keep her away from the bigger dogs; they could eat her for breakfast,' Clive jests.

'She usually gets on well with the other dogs.'

'A bit too well, if you ask me.'

Cassandra gives him a cheeky punch on the arm. 'Aww, Clive, you're a tease.'

'Ouch! That was uncalled for,' he complains, rubbing his injured arm.

All too soon, the morning passes. 'Sorry, guys, I'm off. Some of us must work, you know. Come on, Dexter,' I call with a whistle.

All the dogs stop in their track as Dexter wanders towards me. I rub his ear and fasten the crocodile catch onto his collar. 'Sorry, boy, it's time to go home for lunch.'

At that, he stands alert, ready to go.

'See you again next week,' I say, with an eager dog pulling on the lead.

And So It Began

Daniel Whitehead

Mary Blythe shook out the blanket to get the worst of the water out before hanging it up in the bright sunshine to dry. The afternoon breeze, which came every afternoon off the sea, would help with the drying. It would also clear some of the smell from the uncovered cesspits dotted around the new settlement.

Using the back of her sleeve, she wiped the sweat from her forehead, wishing again that her father had managed to get someone from his monthly trip to Fremantle to help her with her chores. More important, though, had been the wagon and horse which he had bargained for on his last trip. He and Matthew had left the day before, taking a goodly load of timber, which was their most prized resource.

It had been six months since their ship had found the reefs in Cockburn Sound on its maiden journey, delivering her and her father and brother to their new adventure. Her father and brother had helped her onto one of the boats, which had made it to the beach before the ship had departed to nearby Fremantle to effect repairs.

Other ships had left their carcasses in the Sound, and enough of the timber had been rescued to enable a dozen shacks to be built around the bay, of which theirs was the most substantial. Already, it consisted of a separate room for her and a main room with two rough bedrolls, a table, and chairs, and space for the iron stove that her father had planned to obtain on this trip to the settlement.

What was that!

Sudden movement caught her eye, causing her to leave the sheet fluttering in the light breeze and stare into the woods, which still grew quite thick up to half a mile from the beach. *There it is again!* Her heart thumped wildly as she saw about half a dozen pitch black bodies making their way through the edge of the trees and following the stream that ran past her house and in which she had been washing her blankets all morning.

Cautiously, she backed through the opening, leaning the makeshift door closed behind her. Then she shuffled over to the window, peering out to see if the visitors were any closer. Her left hand reached up to grasp the family Bible as if its good words would be enough to fend off any attacks.

Nervously raising her eyes above the sill, she could see in the bright sunshine those alien heathen folk her father had warned her about running in a steady gait along the bank. All six of them were male and carrying long spears, and, she noticed as she lowered her head, her cheeks bright red, all of them were as good as naked with no shame or embarrassment. She cowered down away from the window, trying to read through the good book to take her mind off the sights she had seen as she heard their cheerful voices pass by on the other side of the brook and on down to the sea. She looked out the window again, but taking care not to stare at their bare behinds, she looked out at the other half dozen shacks she could see from her position. No sign of anyone moving could only mean that Elinor was still in bed with croup, and the hunting party was still in the woods somewhere, hoping to catch something for the joint pot.

With plenty of chores to do, Mary had almost forgotten the strange visitors until halfway through the afternoon, when she had almost finished weeding the small vegetable patch and heard a noise behind her. Looking across the stream, she saw five bodies running easily along the path to the woods. Her face reddening once more, she raised her head slightly to see that one of the long spears was resting over the shoulders of two men, its length arched by the weight of five or six large fish spiked through. *At least they will eat well tonight*, she thought with a grimace, wondering what her father would bring from Fremantle in exchange for the lumber they had chopped and stripped over the past month.

A second later, the thought came to her that there had been six before, so she looked cautiously up and saw a bright smile and friendly, bright white eyes in stark contrast to his skin, gazing at her from above the washing on the line. As soon as his eyes met hers, he yelled out an incomprehensible guttural phrase.

In a sudden moment of bravado, Mary tried to repeat the word he had yelled out in a loud but hopefully friendly manner. The character ahead of her gave a cheerful laugh and reached behind his back, pulling from a loose harness a spear about the length of his arm. Halfway up the shaft was a fish that looked like the salmon she remembered from her childhood back in England.

Transfixed by the sight of the potential for a proper meal, she momentarily forgot the dark young man who faced her. Her gaze returned to him as he repeated the word again, but with a questioning lilt to his cadence. The tone did not seem threatening, but aware that this was a savage, and she was a young female alone by all appearances, Mary tried repeating the phrase, but in a more commanding manner.

Not knowing what else to do, Mary ducked below the level of the window on the outer wall and closed her eyes, hoping he would go away.

An hour or more later, she heard the neighing of Belle and the creaking of the wheels as her father and brother negotiated the cart down the path to their shack. By the time they had reached her, she had retrieved the bedding which had dried in the sunshine and found to her surprise the salmon hanging from the line alongside her sheets. The explanation of its appearance was delayed whilst the goods bartered from Fremantle were unpacked and hidden in the shack's cupboards.

Once again, she was thankful to the Lord above that her father had trained in carpentry and lumber work before making the trip to the opposite side of the world. He was also well on the way to training Matthew in the skills necessary to live in this wilderness.

One of his best deals of the day was a large frying pan, which was used for the first time to cook the fish. It was made tastier with the addition of some parsley, which she had brought with her and which she was trying to grow in the garden between the shack and the creek.

***

'Well, that was delicious, Mary,' her father congratulated her on the meal. 'However, I think we need to spend the rest of the evening fastening down everything we can as firmly as possible. By the look of those clouds, we are in for a hell of a blast this night, and I wouldn't be surprised if some of those ships in the harbour come loose before the dawn.'

Mary took a moment to cross herself at her father's brief blasphemy before she heard a blast of a whistle.

Matthew was first out of the shack and looked out to sea to watch as the sails of the East Indiaman came around the headland.

'Isn't that our old ship?' he gasped in wonder as the storm grew in intensity.

'It is, lad, but if you want to be here in the morning give us a hand.'

Her father had one eye out to sea, but the main focus of his attention was on the foundations of their shack. 'Batten down the hatches, as we were always told on board. Get soil up to cover any gaps. I'll nail down anything that looks loose, and we will try to survive the night.'

It took until the darkness overtook them before everything was fastened down to her father's satisfaction. Then all they could do was huddle together and hope it was enough. It took two days before the storm finally broke, and they were finally able to unlatch the door and witness the devastation. Several of the other shacks had come apart, their contents lying nearby.

Out to sea, the worst of the damage was visible. The two smaller ships had almost completely disintegrated, and the ship that had been their home for nearly a year was lying on its side in the shallows, with several bodies floating nearby in the water. The three of them made their way, along with several of their neighbours, to the shore to see if anything could be salvaged. A carved plank of wood, maybe six feet across, tapped against Mary's ankle. With Matthew's help, she lifted it up and turned it over. It was the nameplate of their ship, somehow torn loose in the gale.

'Well,' Mary said, 'we were looking for a new name for our settlement, now that it looks like we will be here permanently. Why don't we call it after the ship that brought us here and that will rest here forevermore? Our new home will be called *Rockingham*. What do you think?'

'As good a name as any,' her father replied with a smile.

A Rocky Past

Georgia Tingley

Sliding from the passenger seat of the rental car, I stood, inhaling the salty sea air fused with the softer fragrance of the frangipani flower I pushed behind my ear. Memories of Rockingham clung to the edges of my mind, and a soft smile flirted with my lips. Scenes of a youth spent picnicking on the foreshore and swimming in the clear turquoise shallows flooded my thoughts and a grin widened my mouth.

'Good times.' My husband of over forty years chuckled, capturing my gaze.

'The best.'

We'd both grown up together in the southern town in the 1970s, went to the same high school and grew up as first friends, then lovers, and eventually spouses.

Rockingham was a coastal holiday town in the late seventies, which meant the trek south was a long but leisurely drive through the southern Perth suburbs. Back then, the Kwinana Freeway ended at Canning Highway. You had to drive towards Fremantle and continue on Stock Road to Rockingham and Mandurah, passing what felt like hundreds of miles of market gardens and grass-tree-covered bush on the journey.

I closed the car door and stepped up onto the lush lawn of Churchill Park. We'd parked close to the main foreshore intersection and hand in hand we sauntered to the 'big tree log.'

'I can't believe this old thing is still here.' Brett slapped the wood with a loving hand. 'You'd think they would have gotten rid of it when they did the makeover.'

Outraged, I turned accusing eyes to him. 'Bite your tongue. This log is a local icon. There would have been an uproar if they'd tried,' I pointed out. 'Anyway, it's probably heritage listed.' My palm smoothed along its surface. 'We'd always climb all over it.' I glanced at the two children walking along its broad body and raised one eyebrow at Brett as if to prove my point.

'Come on, let's take a look at our spot.' He strode off towards the beach.

In the past, we'd often walk to school with some mates and spend the day at the beach. After we all chipped in some money, we'd splurge on a gigantic newspaper-wrapped parcel of hot chips and a bottle of Coke to share.

'Oh God, this brings back memories.' Brett traipsed down the concrete walkway to the small, almost hidden islands of lawn just below the limestone wall. 'Remember hiding in those bushes when we thought the cops would catch us for truancy?'

My smile turned into a gasp. 'Yes! I was petrified of spiders and snakes in there.'

Pulled into a hug, Brett laughed out loud. 'Only harmless Golden Orbs, ya wuss.'

'Harmless to you maybe,' I grouched. 'Let's walk along the path and check out the changes that have been made.' I gazed up at the flock of white birds that screeched and swooped. 'The trees in the park seem taller than before, and surely there weren't these many cockatoos?'

'We have been living overseas for over two decades, there are bound to be some changes,' my husband observed, eagerly climbing the few steps up to a huge round granite sphere that rolled in a massive saucer of water. 'This is new.' He placed both palms on the smooth, wet surface of the ball, spinning it like the children.

'It's interesting.' I joined him, unable to resist placing my hands on the slick stone. 'I forgot how beautiful it is here. No wonder they're building apartments with this fabulous view.'

Brett shook his hands free of water and trailed over to the curved rock wall that overlooked the ocean. 'You know, Talia …' he said when I joined him. 'We could retire here. Lots of great memories and a pretty cruisy lifestyle.'

His gaze on my face was intense, studying the emotions as they flickered in my eyes. 'Yes.' I graced him with a gentle smile. 'I can see us going for beach walks and stopping for lunch at one of the cafés.'

'The grandkids would love it.'

A loud laugh escaped my mouth. 'Wouldn't they? I bet they'd want to move in with Grammy and Pop. We'd be on babysitting duties forever.'

Excitement lit his eyes. 'I could take them fishing. Maybe buy a small boat. We could spend the day at Penguin Island or check out the seals. I wonder if we can still go across to Garden Island?'

'You are keen.' I grinned. 'We need to wait for settlement of our house in Canada first.'

We'd decided to move back home to Perth six months previously. With one daughter here and another who lived in Italy, it seemed pointless being so far away from our family, and especially our grandchildren.

Brett huffed. 'I can't believe we waited so long to come home.' He nudged me in front of him and bracketed me within his arms. 'To think it all started here.'

'Well, it nearly didn't start if your mother had had her way,' I complained, recalling how much she detested me and did her damnedest to keep us apart. Even to the point of moving to the other side of the city.

'Oh God, don't remind me.' My husband laughed. We could, now that she had passed away. But throughout our entire lives, she had never let go of her jealous animosity towards me and made sure I knew it at every opportunity. Eventually, we'd moved our little family overseas, partly to escape from her influence. 'She was a piece of work for sure.'

Snorting, I turned in his arms to face him. 'I can still picture her in her dark green vee-dub beetle, trawling the beaches looking to see if you were with me.'

Brett cringed. 'It was so embarrassing. She'd park up at the trampolines and wait, knowing I'd eventually show up there. My mates used to call her 'the great white,' because she'd circle the park like a shark.'

Rolling my eyes, I threw my head back and hooted. 'That's right, I forgot about her secret nickname. She was well named – any hint of my blood and she was there. To this day, I don't know how she always seemed to know when you were meeting me.'

'Some sort of built-in Talia detector, I reckon,' he sniggered.

We laughed about it now, but that woman nearly broke us up on a couple of occasions. Her hatred ran deep. Bone deep. Not only did she make sure their family moved miles away, but she refused to allow Brett to use the family car to visit me once he'd got his licence. And Brett's father, Charlie, was a spineless coward who would never stand up to her.

'I know I've said this often over the years, but I really appreciate that you didn't give up on me. On us. Nor the way you used to catch a bus, and then the train, and another bus, the journey taking sometimes three hours if the public transport was delayed.' My fingers caressed his stubbled cheek.

'That's how much I loved you,' he preened. 'Still do. Not to mention that your folks would never let me stay the night. Thank goodness for Tommo, or I would have been doing the trip back that night.'

'Also, thank God you bought a car soon.'

Brett stepped back and smiled at a tourist who was taking a photo of the beach vista. He tucked me into his side as we moved on to stroll further down the pathway. 'I saved like crazy, taking any overtime Red Rooster threw my way. Between studying, work, and travelling down to see you, I barely had time to scratch my arse.'

Those early days of struggle seemed like they had happened in a past life. Even to this day, the hostility from his mother still brought a bitter tightness to my chest when I recalled the hurtful words she'd constantly flung in my direction.

'Lucky Evelyn helped you with a loan,' I reminded him.

'Good old Evie. She knew what Mum was like. She'd copped it before she moved out,' Brett reminisced, shaking his head sadly.

Evelyn was Brett's much older only sibling. Twelve years his senior, she had moved out as soon as she could, the toxic environment at home too much for her to handle. With Brett being the change-of-life surprise, his mother rained down all her obsessive love on her 'baby'.

Unfortunately, his sister had died in a car accident in her thirties, which made my mother-in-law even more fixated on her only living child; fixated in an unhealthy and psychotic way. She'd totally poisoned her husband against me, and any family that dared even breathe my name, she'd make sure lived to regret it.

'I sometimes still think about that day at the Rockingham City Shopping Centre when your mum went full-blown nut job on me.' At Brett's look of confusion, I continued. 'Remember, I'd just finished work at Coles and was heading out when I saw your dad sitting in his old Toyota Crown, so I went up to chat with him.'

We strolled along hand in hand towards the Yacht Club, and I could see the frown on my husband's face as he tried to pull up the memory. 'We were laughing at something, I can't recall what now, and Eileen came storming out of the shopping centre shrieking at the top of her lungs to stay away from her man.' I harrumphed in disgust. 'As if I, as a fifteen-year-old teen, would be interested in an old guy like that.'

Brett slapped a hand over his brow in horror. 'Oh hell, I remember now. She was such a jealous fishwife. Completely unhinged at times. You should have seen how enraged she got if a barmaid even smiled at my old man in the pub. There'd be hell to pay for days.'

I shook my head. 'No wonder he just caved and took her side. It was obviously easier than facing her wrath.'

Brett hit the nail on the head when he said Eileen was unhinged. She had some severe mental health issues. Especially in regard to me. Even her own grandchildren weren't spared, disparaging me at every opportunity. She was like a vulture, constantly criticising and picking at me. No … she was worse than a vulture – a vulture at least waits until its prey is dead before it starts to peck away at the carcass.

'Speaking of Rocky City Shops,' Brett said, changing the subject. 'Do you remember when it first opened? I think it was … 1970 or '71, thereabouts. It was the rage out here in the Boonies.'

Grabbing at his arm, I squealed, 'The elephant playground and slide.' We faced each other with goofy grins on our faces. 'It was so lame … yet we thought we were so cool.'

'And that ball thing inside the shops. When they put that in, I would stand there for ages just looking at the mechanics of it.'

'Same.'

'We should check out the shopping centre after lunch,' he grinned wickedly. 'It wouldn't surprise me if they still had it.'

Brett stopped suddenly on the footpath. He turned and cupped my face; a combination of sadness and regret bled from his eyes. 'I'm so sorry, Tal. I know there were some rough times, courtesy of my mum, but some great times too. The important thing is, everything she did or tried to do – it didn't work. We've spent our life happy together – in spite of her. Or perhaps to spite her and her machinations. And I'm going to grow old with you here in Rockingham.' He brushed his lips over mine in a soft kiss of promise.

'We will.' I beamed at him. 'Let's not ruin our day talking about her and our rocky past.' I laced my fingers with Brett's. 'I saw a restaurant on the corner overlooking the ocean. Shall we grab some lunch then take a drive past our old houses?'

'Sounds like a plan.' My husband grinned in delight. 'I bet my house has been knocked down and a million units built in its place. Our block was huge.'

Our steps quickened. 'Oh, and we should take a drive along the coast too. I want to see what Point Peron looks like, and Penguin Island too. I wonder if people still walk over the sandbar.' Pleasure and excitement lit our hearts as we set off to pursue our new Rocky future.

A Whale in the Bay

Teena Raffa-Mulligan

Some people are bird spotters. It makes their day if they catch sight of a particular bird.

I spot dolphins. The sight of one of these beautiful creatures thrills me. It makes my day. If I happen to see a pod frolicking – as happened one early morning when I had the rare privilege of sharing the ocean with about a dozen, including youngsters – the delight can last for days.

So as a dolphin spotter of many years' experience, whenever I'm walking along the beach path near our Warnbro home, I stop to scan the ocean.

While swimming in our beautiful bay, I check periodically to see whether I have the company of dolphins. It doesn't matter how far away they are, just knowing they're there is enough.

One summer when the grandchildren were still young, my older daughter and her family headed over the hill with us to the beach. I was scanning for dolphins as usual. I noticed immediately there was something different that day. A few hundred metres offshore where the ocean changes colour, a big dark shape protruded from the water.

'What's that?' I wondered aloud.

'A rock,' said my daughter, who was less familiar with 'our beach'.

No. Rocks that big didn't appear overnight.

Suddenly, a huge tail rose out of the water, a trademark spurt hosed skywards, and the mystery was solved. A lone whale was basking in the bay, remarkably close to shore. We thrilled at the sight. It was awesome.

Excitement buzzed along the beach and people of all ages hurried to the top of the sand dunes to better view this unexpected visitor. It's the only time I've seen a whale in our bay.

I still scan the ocean for my friends the dolphins and feel that wonderful lift of spirits when a grey shape curves out of the water. Maybe one day I'll be lucky enough to experience the wonder of another visiting whale in the bay.

Sometimes, though, I do wonder why there's not the same thrill of pleasure at ants, for instance, or the humble housefly. Yet are they less of a miracle than dolphins or a whale in the bay? That's a point to ponder.

Changing Times

Teena Raffa-Mulligan

Jane managed to keep it together until the side door closed on the mobile vet and another era of her life. Her anguished wail drowned out the sound of the van heading out of the drive. Collapsing onto the kitchen floor with her back against the cupboards, she gave way to convulsive sobs. She couldn't stop them if she tried. Pain sliced through her, deep and raw.

Bess was gone. Anyone who said, 'It's just a pet,' had no idea of how much the gentle chocolate Labrador had meant to Jane. She'd been her lifeline in those dark days after Matt's fatal heart attack twelve months ago. Her reason for getting out of bed each morning in those empty, numbing days immediately afterwards. Her companion through the too-quiet days and lonely nights that followed. And a ready excuse to delay giving in to Kelli's urging, 'Move closer to us, Mum. We're worried about you being down here in Rockingham all on your own.'

'Bess wouldn't cope with a shift,' she'd said. 'Not at her age. Not with her anxieties. She doesn't like change.'

Kelli knew her mum didn't like change either.

And now Bess was gone too. Her beautiful canine companion with the liquid honey eyes and the sweet nature. Jane let the tears flow unchecked.

The warmth of the day gave way to evening's chill as she sat on the cold tiles, back propped against the cupboard door. At last, the tears dried up and, cold and stiff, she used the edge of the bench to pull herself up off the floor. As if on autopilot, she removed everything of Bess's from the house, including the unused food, and shoved it all into the bin. How could she face any reminder of her absence? It had almost broken her to have everything of Matt's in the house in the weeks following his death.

That done, and with no appetite for dinner, she crawled into bed, hoping for the oblivion of sleep, but an onslaught of memories kept it at bay until exhaustion claimed her in the still dark hours before dawn. She slept fitfully, waking often at the imagined sound of Bess's toenails clicking along the passage tiles or the gentle rhythm of her snores inside the bedroom. Realisation triggered renewed sobs, and she reached even now across the bed for the comfort of Matt's absent embrace. He'd understand. He'd loved Bess too.

She woke to daylight in a tangle of bedclothes and Bess's 'breakfast is late' bark. No. Not Bess, the phone. Loss slammed her once more. She rubbed her eyes and reached for her glasses in the bedside cabinet, saw it was Kelli and took a deep breath before answering the call.

'Hello, darling, are you on your way to work?'

'Yes, unfortunately,' and she launched into an account of the latest chaos caused by her office manager, who apparently couldn't do anything right, so Kelli might as well do the job herself.

Jane thought she'd been responding appropriately till her daughter stopped mid-sentence and asked, 'Are you okay, Mum?'

Jane was about to say yes – she didn't want to worry Kelli, spoil her concentration while she was driving – but instead her voice broke on the words, 'Bess is gone.'

'Oh Mum, I'm so sorry. We know how much you loved her. Look, how about I pick you up after work and bring you here for a few days. You might be best to have some company.'

The last thing Jane felt like was being fussed over and treated like fragile china that might shatter at any moment. 'There's no need. Don't worry about me, I'll be fine. You'd best get yourself to work.'

'If you're sure…'

'I am,' Jane said firmly and ended the call.

Distraction got her through the day. A complete cleanout and reorganisation of the pantry. Sweeping up the fallen leaves behind the shed. An energetic ride on the exercise bike because today wasn't the day for a brisk walk along the beach path where so many of the regulars knew her and Bess.

Pretence helped, as it had in the aftermath of Matt's passing, when she'd told herself he was simply out in the shed tinkering about, or had taken a long drive along the coastline. Imagining that Bess, too, was still around, snoozing in the next room or foraging for olives among the trees, eased the pain.

'Day One done,' she said aloud in the quiet kitchen just past six o'clock after an early shower. 'Nothing for you, Bess,' she said automatically as she opened a can of tuna and fetched a slice of bread to toast. Tears pricked. She brushed them away.

Footsteps sounded on the front porch, a key turned in the security door, and Brad called, 'Hi, Ma. Only me.'

He stopped in the kitchen. 'You're in your PJs.'

'I wasn't expecting anyone.'

'I had a job in Port Kennedy. Thought I'd call past.' He nodded towards the can of tuna and the loaf of bread on the counter. 'Looks like I timed it well. Me and Tasha are going for Thai and thought you might like to join us.'

'You've been talking to your sister.'

He gave the crooked grin that was so like his father's and ran a hand through his close-cropped hair – heaven forbid he'd let the curls grow.

'Yeah. Well, uh, we thought you could use some company, seeing as Bess…' His voice trailed away, and his gaze shifted to the empty space her dog bed usually occupied.

Tears filled Jane's eyes and slid down her cheeks. She turned away. In an instant, her tall, strong son's arms were around her. 'Come on, Ma. Get yourself dressed. Let's get you out of the house for a bit.'

'That's a lovely offer, darling, but do you mind if I say no? I've worked myself to a standstill. I just need to tuck myself in front of the telly, then get an early night.'

'Whatever you want, Ma. But forget tuna on toast. I'll order you Thai online, have a cuppa with you while we wait for it to be delivered, then leave you to your quiet night. And don't forget, we're only a phone call away if you need us.'

In the days that followed, Kelli checked in daily. Brad called past when he was in the area.

'You don't need to do this,' Jane said at last.

'We care.'

'I know you do. But you've just got to let me get on with it. I'll be okay.'

'But will you, Mum? You're on your own in that big house. It's a lot to look after. What if something happens? You're seventy-eight. There's no one there with you.'

'We had this conversation when your dad died. I'll know when it's time to make the move.'

'If you're worried about it being too much...feel like it's all too hard...well, we'll look after everything. Get the house ready to put it on the market. It'll sell in a snap in the current market. You'll get a good price, be able to get yourself into something better suited to what you need now.'

'And you know what that is?' Jane snapped.

She was never sharp with her adult children. It took Kelli by surprise. 'Sorry.'

The awkward silence extended between them. Jane took a breath. 'Look, I know you have my best interests at heart. But I'm still capable of looking after myself and running my own life. Please let me do that. I know you're all there if I need you. And I'll let you know when I do.'

'OK. Talk to you tomorrow.' The tremble in Kelli's voice showed she was upset.

Jane's stomach felt knot-tied. A walk along the beach path would help. She stopped at her usual spot to appreciate the view of the bay. She loved this place, her home for the past thirty years. Could she leave, say goodbye to it? She breathed in the sea air, stared out over the bay, tranquil today, sunlight shimmering the water. A soft breeze caressed her face, lifting her hair, swaying the coastal grasses. She'd seen this stretch of ocean in all its moods. Welcomed its healing solace in times of loss and grief, revelled in the sights and sounds of sea and shore when gladness filled her heart. There was nowhere else that connected so deeply. Yes, it would be a joy to see more of family. But start over? At her age? Leave behind her yoga and art classes, the monthly book club, her circle of friends, the familiarity of her neighbourhood shopping centre.

Stay or go? The question beat time with every footstep of her walk along the path, and persisted on her return home.

'It's a dilemma,' she said aloud, adding her sunhat to the stand in the entry, replacing her sunglasses with the everyday multifocals she'd left on the hall table.

She straightened the carnations in their vase, still in bloom from the bouquet Kelli had brought the previous weekend, and sighed. The walk along the beach path had not provided the hoped-for clarity.

'What should I do, Matt? And you, Bess, what do you think, old girl?'

Silence wrapped around her. The house was still and quiet.

Jane shook her head. Really? Asking for guidance from the dead. Was that what she'd come to? Kelli was probably right. It was time to move on.

Urgent knocking on the screen door halted her musings, and Jane spun round to see a small girl on the porch, flush-faced and breathless, flyaway fair hair escaping lopsided pigtails.

Jane flung open the door, accident scenarios instantly coming to mind. 'My goodness, what is it?'

But the child grinned – not an emergency, then – and looked up at her expectantly. 'I need to get toffee and candy.'

Jane frowned. It wasn't Halloween. 'I don't have toffee or candy.'

The child shook her head impatiently. 'Out your back.'

Stranger and stranger, as Alice would have said.

'Who are you?' asked Jane.

'Melia. Not A-melia.'

'And where do you live, Melia not Amelia?'

'Round the corner. Behind your place.'

Now they were getting somewhere. She'd heard the old man had died and a family had moved in. This must be one of the children she'd heard playing in the yard.

'Does your mum know you're here?'

'Ollie does. He jumped over the fence. I told him not to. We should knock and ask. Now can I get toffee and candy?' Her face suddenly brightened as if she'd remembered something important. 'Please!' she added with a satisfied grin.

The encounter was beginning to make sense. A sudden shout of 'Gotcha!' from the backyard filled in the final puzzle piece.

'Come on then,' said Jane, and led the way through the house and out into the back garden. A boy who looked to be a few years older than the girl was standing amongst the trees and shrubs nursing a large rabbit.

'Oh good, he's got Toffee,' said Melia. A small hen emerged from the shrubbery and ran across the lawn, flapping its wings and squawking. 'Candy!' she cried. Diving on the runaway, she scooped it up and held it close to her chest, shaking her head. 'Naughty, naughty girl.'

Jane raised an eyebrow at her unexpected visitors. 'Are any more of your pets hiding in my garden waiting to surprise me?'

'Buster wanted to dig his way in too, but I shut him in the laundry,' said the boy.

That explained the persistent barking.

'Ah. Very sensible of you. Well, I'm guessing there's a gap in the fence?'

'Yup. I'll show you. Here, hold Toffee.' He thrust the rabbit at Jane, and she had no choice but to take the squirming creature. Then he crawled in behind the large bushy grevillea in the corner of the yard and held one of the lower branches aside to reveal where a corner of the fence had broken away. A freshly dug hole had widened the gap to allow entry to the intruders.

Ollie backed out onto the grass and dusted himself down. 'We can put Toffee and Candy back in our place and fill in the hole, but I think they'll be back.'

'Agreed,' said Jane. 'We need to do a fix-it job. There's some bits and pieces of wood in the shed that should do the trick for now. I'll fetch them. Hold tight to your pets. Don't let them escape.'

Twenty minutes later, the escapees had been thrust back into their own yard, and the gap in the fence was securely blocked off with a large piece of chipboard and several limestone bricks.

Jane took the children indoors to wash their hands, gave them a banana and a glass of apple juice, then helped them back over the fence into their own yard. As their lively chatter faded away, Jane stood in her garden, smiling. What an unexpected interlude.

Several days later, Jane was out the back tending to the vegie patch when she heard the murmur of voices from among the branches of the tree closest to the fence in the children's yard.

'She's outside.'

'I'm going over.'

'Me too.'

She was about to have visitors.

Ollie swung from an overhanging branch and dropped to the ground among the bushes on her side of the fence. About to follow suit, Melia released one arm, then lost confidence and grabbed back at the branch. 'Catch me!'

'Wait!' called Jane.

Before she had a chance to stand up, Ollie was wrapping his arms around his sister's legs and easing her safely to the ground. She cartwheeled across the lawn and came to a breathless halt in front of Jane.

'Candy laid an egg,' she said.

'Did you have it for breakfast?'

'No, Mummy's going to make a cake after work.'

'You won't want to try any of my choc chip muffins, then.'

'I do.' Melia giggled and danced off to smell the daisies that were a mass of colour beneath the trees.

Ollie squatted beside Jane. He watched her for a few moments, then asked, 'What are you doing?'

She indicated the row of carrots she'd sown several weeks ago. 'Carrot seeds are really tiny and it's not possible to plant each one separately so I scatter them and wait till they start to grow. See how closely they're growing together? If I left them like that there'd be no room for the carrots to grow, so I go along and weed out the smallest ones. It's calling thinning them out. Those that are left will have the space they need to grow strong straight roots.'

Ollie looked thoughtful. 'How did you know to do it that way?'

'My grandfather showed me. His whole backyard was a vegie patch when I was growing up.'

'Our granddad died.' Melia, a daisy tucked behind one ear, had wandered back to see what they were doing.

'Yes,' said Jane. 'It's sad when someone dies.'

Ollie shrugged. 'We didn't really know him. Mum said we came to see him once when I was little but I don't remember.'

'I wasn't born yet.' Melia had lost interest in the vegie patch and was sitting on one of the patio chairs swinging her legs to and fro.

Ollie inspected the rest of the vegetables, wanting to know what each plant was, marvelling at the tiny cucumbers and capsicums, the green tomatoes. 'I might like to grow stuff to eat, now we've got a yard,' he said.

Using the kneeling frame for support, Jane rose and dusted herself down. 'I've got an idea, Ollie, come with me.'

She led the way to the shed, where she fetched a large plastic pot and the bag of leftover potting mix. 'Let's get your garden started. I'll give you a couple of cherry tomato bushes.'

'Really? To take home?' Ollie's eyes shone.

'Of course. You'll need to look after them. What about you, Melia? Do you want to grow something too?'

Melia had stopped in front of the easel Jane hadn't been near in months. 'Oh,' she breathed. 'It's a fire.'

'Do you think so?' Jane came to stand beside her, studying the canvas with its fluid interplay of vibrant reds, oranges, yellows and deep, dark purple. 'I pour the paint on and see how it flows. I haven't done any for a long time. Perhaps you'd like to do some with me one day?'

Melia nodded enthusiastically. 'I like painting.' She paused. 'And muffins.'

Jane laughed. 'Let's get this potted garden sorted for Ollie and then we'll go indoors and have afternoon tea.'

By the time the children had climbed back over the fence with the help of a strategically placed patio chair, Jane knew they'd been living in a tiny Sydney apartment till 'Granddad left us his house', their mum was a nurse now working at the local hospital, and they didn't see their dad because 'he lives in New Zealand with his new family'.

'See you tomorrow,' called Ollie.

'Me too!'

Jane stood in the garden listening to their receding footsteps and the raucous greeting from their dog as they went indoors, a woman's voice asking, 'What mischief have you two been up to?'

She smiled. Life was full of surprises. Losing Matt and Bess had left such an empty space in her life. That hadn't changed. But two children had brought an unexpected ray of sunshine into the grey days. She'd tidy the kitchen, then walk around the corner to introduce herself to their mum. She'd want to know who Jane was, especially as Melia wanted to come and paint a picture and Ollie wanted to learn about growing vegies. Later, decided Jane, she'd call Kelli and Brad, let them know she would move when the time felt right. It wasn't yet.

Coming Home

Karlene Jolliffe

'Back here by nine or you'll be sleeping with the seagulls!'

The driver laughs heartily as the twenty or so retirees clamber from the bus. In stark contrast with the sterile, chilly air-conditioning endured on the hour-long trip, the hot air, laden with the scent of salt, pine and peppermint, draws murmurs of delight.

'Okay, folks, gather round,' the driver continues, gesturing for everyone to move closer. 'There's a footpath here next to the beach, one over the road along the café strip, and one smack down the middle through the park. They all end up at the beach plaza and boardwalk where you'll find more dinner options, a grog shop if you want BYO, and a couple of ice cream shops if you fancy afters. This is the Wanliss Street car park, and this is where I'll pick you up. It's about seven hundred metres from here to the plaza, and another hundred to the end of the boardwalk, so make sure you allow enough time to get back. Enjoy your evening in Rockingham, ladies and gentlemen.'

The seniors give cheerio waves as the bus pulls away. Couples and groups of three and four disperse, most heading up the chunky limestone steps to the footpath overlooking the beach. The rest go across the road to examine the northernmost restaurants and bars lodged on ground floors of multi-storey apartment buildings.

Lionel lingers in the car park until everyone has gone, then sets off through the park. It's a striking green space filled with mature eucalypts, peppermints and Norfolk pines. The absence of the Fremantle Doctor—the renowned Western Australian summer sea breeze—means the heat is stifling, but the leafy canopy fends off most of the sun's direct assault.

He's astounded at the number of people out and about late on a midweek afternoon. Kiddies play in sandpits containing climbing frames, slides and swings while parents and grandparents watch from rugs and folding chairs set on the lush, mown grass. Singles and couples winding down at the end of the day relax on bench seats and gaze out over the ocean, Fremantle a hazy speck on the horizon. Joggers glistening with sweat pound the pavement, while dogs lead their owners at a more leisurely pace. Even half a dozen people clad in wetsuits lug scuba diving paraphernalia across the park to explore the underwater world of the bay.

A small car park briefly interrupts the never-ending stretch of green. Needing to catch his breath, Lionel looks around for somewhere to sit, and four wide limestone steps at the end of the car park beckon. At the top is some sort of circular sculpture overlooking the beach, and off to the side is a vacant bench seat. The sculpture, Lionel discovers to his amazement, is what must be a several-tonne smooth ball of rock revolving slowly on a microfilm of water flowing between it and a perfectly-matched stone basin.

Gratefully, he lowers his body onto the seat, squinting against the sun, which is well into its descent. A man and a woman, about half his age, toddle up from the beach and park themselves next to him. Lionel nods in response to their greetings then looks away.

'Magnificent, isn't it?' says the man.

The beach? The park? The view? Perhaps he's referring to the bountiful supply of cafés and restaurants. Or apartments and penthouses. Maybe he simply means the floating rock ball. It's all impressive, but it's not what Lionel has come for. What *has* he come for? Did he really expect to find the modest seaside settlement of his youth? The unhurried, uncomplicated town that gifted him the best years of his life?

'Apparently, Rockingham used to be a real dump,' the man goes on. 'Decades ago, that is,' he qualifies. 'But the council's done a fantastic job and now it's a true gem of a place. We moved here four years ago and wouldn't live anywhere else. There's everything here you could want.'

Lionel stares at the horizon. Not everything. Not anymore. He shouldn't have come. He should have thrown the flyer in the bin and stayed home, like he always did. But the date had hit him with a jolt. Sixty years to the day when a future filled with love and happiness had instead become a lifetime of bitterness and regret. But did he want to stay an angry old man? Maybe it was time to return to the place he'd never wanted to leave and lay the past to rest. But how does one let go if there's nothing left to let go of?

The couple heads off, and Lionel also gets to his feet. It's far too hot to walk in the sun, but he does it anyway, continuing along the footpath overlooking the beach. White sand stretches away in both directions, and children and adults alike paddle in the small, lazy waves or float in the clear, shallow water. Further out, where the water turns deep blue, what appear to be teenagers jump off a pontoon. Homework and chores, it seems, aren't the foremost after-school activities anymore.

With the sun full in his face and people and dogs passing in both directions, the footpath commands his attention, and it's not until he's under the shade of a tree in the middle of an expansively paved area that he looks around properly. With oddly-shaped coloured seating, a weird piece of artwork, and a mix of business, retail and restaurants, this must be the plaza. He's pleasantly surprised to recognise the adjoining road intersection, now partly blocked off to create this space, but it's impossible to correlate any of the surrounding infrastructure with what stood here six decades ago.

Crossing the plaza, he sets off along the boardwalk. On the ocean side are terraced grass areas, a children's play area, shade umbrellas and more seating. On the other side, single-level apartments sit atop yet another string of restaurants, justifiably popular due to their open frontages and views of Garden Island and the setting sun. He spots a group of village residents already settled and clinking glasses across a table.

Finally, he reaches the last of the clipped lawn areas, the last of the buildings, and the last of the paving. A plain concrete footpath leads on around the less developed shoreline of the bay, but he's come far enough, for here, at the end of the boardwalk, Rockingham finally offers up a glimpse of the past. The Cruising Yacht Club of Western Australia, albeit in a clubhouse far more modern than he'd known, still stands proud, a sentinel keeping watch over the whole of Cockburn Sound. And, out in front, adorned with small boats and recreational anglers, is the jetty, and although now a robust formation of concrete and metal, recollecting the creaking wooden structure of his youth takes no effort at all.

Lionel sets his weary body down on a seat just on from the yacht club. A young woman is playing with a toddler on the grass about twenty metres away, and he watches for a moment then closes his eyes against the sun's dazzling reflection across the water. What now? How do you release the past and *move on*?

The seat shifts slightly as someone sits beside him. Startled, he opens his eyes and looks around, but it's a few seconds before his vision adjusts. 'Iris?' he whispers. Silly old fool. The heat has addled his brain. He should have brought a bottle of water with him. He looks away, looks back. She's still there, smiling at him.

'Hello, Leo.' That's what she'd always called him. *Leo, my lion with an 'el'* she'd always said.

He's dumbfounded. 'But how——?' He shakes his head. 'I can't believe it.'

She sits, poised, hands folded gracefully in her lap. She's aged and greyed like him, but sixty years has done nothing to diminish her beauty. 'It's wonderful to see you,' she says, then looks out over the water. 'It's going to be an amazing sunset.'

Lionel follows her gaze, squinting at the horizon. The sun is flexing and shimmering as it hovers above the fusion of water and sky. His skin is burning, but he's not about to move. 'I didn't know you were still in Rockingham,' he says, eyes on the skyline.

'I never left,' she says simply. Unlike him.

'Well, the place has certainly changed,' he remarks lightly, trying to mask his bewilderment at this astonishing situation. 'I hardly recognise anything. It's nothing like when we——'

Darn it! Should he talk about the past? Should he talk about *them*? Did he want to? And what about Iris? Did her memories of so long ago cause her pain? Or did that life mean nothing to her anymore?

She slips her hand into his. 'It's okay, Leo,' she says, as if reading his mind. 'It's all okay.'

He searches her face, sees only tenderness and sincerity, and the words come tumbling out. 'Iris, I'm so sorry.' His voice is thick with emotion. 'Your father—I went to see him and he wouldn't—he told me to stay away. He said I wasn't good enough. He said I wasn't...' He hesitates and swallows, his Adam's apple bobbing painfully. 'He said I wasn't the right *class*.'

Lionel turns away. How can he ever let go when her father's words cut as deeply now as they had then? Iris squeezes his hand, and he turns back to her. 'I couldn't bear the thought of not being with you,' he says miserably. 'And to see you with someone else, well, that would've been the end of me.' His shoulders slump. 'I had to leave.'

'I know,' she says.

He looks down and runs his thumb lightly over her fingers. When he looks up, his eyes are brimming. 'I was going to ask you to marry me.'

'I know,' she says again.

They sit in silence, watching the sun kiss the horizon. The woman on the grass glances around and Lionel manages a feeble smile but she's already looking away.

'I saw your wedding photo in the paper,' he says valiantly. 'You looked lovely. And your husband looked like a fine man.'

'Charlie.' Iris smiles and nods. 'Yes, he was a good man. He passed on a few years ago now.'

'I'm sorry. Do you have children?'

She shakes her head. 'It wasn't meant to be.'

'I don't either,' he says. 'I never married,' he adds quietly.

She squeezes his hand again, and the heaviness in his heart lifts just a little. Shifting slightly to ease the ache in his back, Lionel gives a nod in the direction of the boardwalk. 'Remember the trampolines that were up there? And the fun fair with the bumper cars?'

Iris laughs delightedly. 'I do! And the mini golf. And the roller skating.'

Lionel groans. 'I'd rather not remember the roller skating. I always went home with bruises from top to tail. You were okay, though.'

Iris raises her eyebrows. '*Okay?*'

'Oh, all right, you were pretty good,' he concedes. 'Really, really good!' he adds quickly as her eyebrows go higher. They laugh, holding tight to each other's hand. The young woman looks around again but quickly turns away.

'You were good at the mini golf,' says Iris. 'Although I did beat you a couple of times,' she adds playfully.

'You didn't beat me,' Lionel huffs, feigning indignation. 'I was being a gentleman. I let you win.'

'Of course you did,' she giggles. 'What else do you remember?'

He remembers everything. 'Eating fish and chips on the beach.'

'Oh, yes!' she exclaims. 'Wrapped in newspaper, with lots of vinegar. Soggy but so good. What else?'

'The building that was on the corner with the tea rooms and the dance hall.'

'The Trocadero,' she says dreamily. 'We had fun there, didn't we? It was a real shame when they pulled it down. That was nearly twenty years ago now. What else?'

He could go on forever, but shakes his head. 'Your turn,' he says. 'What do you remember?'

Iris ponders, then, 'Sundays in the beer garden.'

Lionel bursts out laughing. 'Of all the things, you pick the hotel?'

'It wasn't just a hotel,' she quips. 'It had the lawns and the roses and the pond. It was all so pretty.'

'You're right,' he agrees. 'It was.'

'And they had those beautiful swans that lived on the pond,' she muses. 'Two black and two white. Actually,' she grins impishly, 'I seem to recall someone getting a bit too close...'

Lionel makes a face. 'It might be funny now, but it certainly wasn't back then. That blasted thing scared the life out of me!'

'I know, I know.' She strokes his hand soothingly, but her shoulders twitch with silent laughter. 'Actually, it *was* funny back then,' she teases.

They sit comfortably, immersed in their own thoughts. The sun melts into the ocean, transforming the water into a mass of sparkling gold. The woman with the toddler looks over once more, and Lionel hopes they aren't being annoying by talking and laughing too loudly. Maybe she finds them amusing, two old people behaving like teenagers. He doesn't mind. He doesn't mind about anything.

'What about the jetty?' asks Iris quietly, almost shyly. 'After the yacht club. Do you remember that?'

Lionel turns, and his gaze lingers on her face. 'Of course I remember,' he says, his voice husky with emotion. 'Kissing the most beautiful girl in the world on her eighteenth birthday.' He smiles ruefully. 'The day I thought you'd be mine forever. Sixty years ago today. Happy birthday, Iris.'

The sun slips out of sight and the glorious Rockingham sunset unfolds—red, orange and yellow blazing across the sky. At last, something from the past unchanged after all these years. But so too, he realises, is his love for the girl in front of him. He's been such a fool, sixty years clinging to the memory of what he'd lost instead of what he'd had.

Every detail of that night is vivid in his mind—her dark, wavy hair cascading over her shoulders, her flawless skin luminescent under the clubhouse lighting, her laughter as they spin on the dance floor, the moonlight on her face as he holds her in his arms at the end of the jetty. All the bitterness of the past—her father's refusal to give her hand in marriage, having to return the ring, leaving everything behind—none of it matters anymore. And so, in this place, in this moment in time, he lets it go.

Iris lifts her hand to his cheek and he leans into her touch. 'It's time to go,' she says softly.

Turning his face, he presses a kiss to her palm. 'Remarkable,' he murmurs against her hand, closing his eyes as contentment washes over him. 'I feel like I'm home.'

'Leo, my lion,' says Iris tenderly, and he feels what could be the light touch of her lips on his cheek. 'My darling, you *are* home.'

***

The woman shifts the toddler to her other hip and pulls more tissues from her bag. Her cheeks are flushed, mascara smudged beneath her eyes.

'In the beginning,' she recounts, 'he seemed so sad. But at the end,' she dabs her eyes and gives a watery smile. 'I've never seen anyone so happy. The more he talked, the happier he was.'

Startled, the policewoman looks up from her notebook. 'He was talking to someone? There was someone else there?'

The woman looks over at the empty seat and shakes her head. 'No. It was just him. There was nobody else there.'

En route

Teena Raffa-Mulligan

'Let's go for a bike ride,' said the Man Around the House. I didn't need much convincing. What a great way to start the day. Soon after sunrise, we took to the road and headed for the beach path that meanders along the coast near our Warnbro home. The surroundings had that soft look of a new day when the brighter light of a higher sun has not yet sharpened the edges. Birds were just beginning to wake and sing the day a welcome. There was a touch of freshness to the air, along with the fleeting fragrance of bush blossoms.

The bike path is great for exercise, offering plenty of variety between flat, easy stretches, testing hills, cruisy slopes, gentle curves and, occasionally, a sharper bend that requires full attention to avoid running down unwary pedestrians approaching from the opposite direction. As I cycled along, it occurred to me that life's pretty much like our early morning bike ride along the beach path. One minute you can be cruising happily along, the next minute you're trying to avoid the jolts and bumps on the road ahead.

There's no way to see what's around the next corner, so you have to pay attention to where you're going. Lose focus, drift off into a daydream, and a spill could result. Look too far ahead, though, and whatever is on the road directly ahead will be missed. Don't look back, or you'll come a cropper.

As we travel our life path, we don't know the precise route or the length of the journey. We do know our final destination, and there are other certainties.

The path will not always be smooth. There will be bumps to negotiate, hills to climb, and sometimes it will take all our effort and determination to keep going.

Pushing uphill against the wind is damned hard work. It's a case of 'grit the teeth and just keep going'. But always there's the knowledge that if we get over that hump, the downhill coast will be a cruise.

And there's nothing that quite matches the exhilaration of freewheeling with the wind behind you and a song in your heart. You've done it, met a challenge. And who cares if you don't know what's around the next bend? That's the adventure.

It's years since we took that early morning bike ride together. These days I head off along the beach path on foot. It hasn't lost its magic — and as I follow the winding route from home and back, I am reminded that wherever we are on our life journey, now is all we have. Not tomorrow or next year or a decade down the track.

It's this moment that matters. Make it count. Live it to the max. Sadness or gladness. Anger or laughter. Experience it. Feel it. Then let it go. It's passed. And it is the past. Be present.

Farmer's Retreat

Lia Eliades

The old Rockingham shack leans and yawns, like an open mouth. You can see outside from the inside, and you can see the sun setting. Shafts of light enter uninvited; the odd rat too. The kitchen rains in a line from the fridge to the cupboard, each pop rivet of the roof line rusted, allowing the tears of all the losses to enter the house, to remind me that this is all that is left from ten thousand hectares and fourteen thousand sheep to the tiny asbestos shack. Batten and boards glued together here, hammered shut there.

Gated like a fortress to prevent the yearly burglaries that used to take place each winter, when we were on the farm planting the crops and feeding the sheep; we would come back, only to find a missing fridge, TV gone again. Year after year, new appliances — not a bad caper, really, until the insurance company got tired of replacing our white goods. So now we are hemmed in by gates and window guards made by a farmer with no aesthetic flair – caged like the animals we used to keep, cramped quarters stuffed with fifty-eight years' worth of living, loving, and dying.

The trees are the saving grace; they lift and float. The pepper trees gently stroke at the windows and the rusting roof, sometimes lashing out, cat of nine tails punishing, again and again. And when the storm passes and the rain stops, and the kitchen no longer cries, the kookaburras laugh and the Maggies throat-sing like Mongolian nomads calling out in lonely valleys to no one in particular.

It is safe to go outside and take refuge under the shade of the magnificent gum tree, the volunteer lilac trees and the pepper trees. They protect you from the sun that has no filter, the brutal light of reality that means to harm, but the trees … they can take it. They take it all: the glare, the flare, and turn it into oxygen and green grass and birdsong and wind and warmth and dappled spots of light, letting me know that somehow everything will be all right again.

Flowers

Rosanne Dingli

They sat on the timber jetty, the three of them swinging their legs, barefooted and wearing new bathing suits. Poppy would have preferred a blue one, a blue bikini, but they nearly always wore what their mum chose.

'I know your styles, girls; I know your figures. I know what's appropriate for your ages ... and I won't have you showing off your midriffs to anyone with the gall to stare!'

'Mum ... who in all of Rockingham will stare at us? Born here, schooled here, with most of our things bought here. *Boring!* Mary was always forthright, but she always stopped when her mother glared, her 'Carnaby Crimson' lips drawn into a grim straight line. Someone should tell their mother: the darker the lipstick, the smaller the mouth looks to everyone, except her own eyes in the mirror.

Rose swung her feet and looked down at the shallow water below them. 'Time for another dip?'

'Time for an ice cream, but ...'

'We won't get all the way there and all the way back and still be in time to shower before tea.' Poppy hauled herself up and pulled on a terry-towelling shift. 'I've thought of something. Do you know how old we'll be at the turn of the century?'

'What century? What do you mean?' Rose was looking for something at the bottom of her bag.

'When the nineteen-hundreds finish, dopey, it will be the year two thousand. A new *millenium*.' Poppy sniffed, and squashed on a straw hat. 'And I'll be forty-seven.'

'What!'

'Never!'

Poppy grinned at them and giggled. 'Now think what that means.' She looked Rose and Mary in the face. 'Think!'

Mary was not listening. A gaggle of boys had just come onto the jetty.

'First dip of the season, Martin girls? Got any of those toes wet?' They gave adolescent laughs. 'Or those legs? Or those swimsuits?'

Poppy and Rose laughed back, exchanging ribbing and short stabbing sentences with the boys they knew very well from a childhood at primary school. But Mary retreated, staring every now and then at a dark-haired boy of about her age, whose wide grin and freckles across shoulders and nose spoke of a life spent outdoors.

The girls moved towards the footpath as the boys walked onward along the jetty, and Mary looked back.

'You'll only change two letters of your name if you marry Harry Maslin, Mary!' Her sisters teased her all the way to Fisher Street. 'Mum says you mustn't *stare*!' They tormented her all the way round the corner to their neat house on the corner of Samuel Street.

'I got what it means.' Mary spoke at last, just outside the back door on the veranda. 'The millenium thing?' No one heard her.

They weren't to get a speck of sand inside, so had to leave their things on the hooks out there and dust themselves down. Rose uncoiled part of the hose and turned the tap. 'Ouch! That first bit's always so *hot*! Feet, come on, rinse your feet. Wait, it's still hot!'

'Hot like Harry Maslin! Hot like Harry Maslin!' They sang out, Rose and Poppy together.

'*Girls!* You're not being vulgar, are you? Mary, come and toss a salad. Poppy, you shower first. Rose, pop those towels in the laundry ... they've been to the beach twice!'

'It means I'll be forty-nine!' Mary's train of thought was not punctured, either by her sisters' teasing or her mother's constant instruction.

***

'I thought you liked May Street, Mary.' Harry's face showed his disappointment. He had worked hard to get Mary all she desired, or so he thought. He rubbed the bridge of his nose, where his teenage freckles had all but disappeared.

'I've always wanted a corner house. You know, like we had as girls. And our Michael will be closer to the high school if we move out to Safety Bay.'

'What's wrong with Rockingham High School?'

Mary's mouth became a straight line, very much like her mother's. Harry thought of Mrs Martin. She was a battleaxe. He hoped Mary was not turning into one.

'Marigold ... come on, Marigold!' He very rarely called her that these days. There was a day he would laugh about the sisters all having flower names. He used to tease her about wanting to be different and insisting on plain Mary.

'Poppy and Rose both live out that way.'

'*Out that way!* Poppy lives in a shack in Singleton, all year round! The place is as draughty as a church. I reckon she'll have to be back to look after your mother soon. She's no longer young, your mum. But that shack. That's not what you want.'

'You know what I mean, Harry. I don't want a glorified holiday home, a tizzied-up beach shack.' She waved a hand around and flapped and snapped a tea towel and started to polish glasses she had already shined.

'You want a big grand house like Rose's, on that rise in Warnbro. Do you really want to live in the middle of a bare, dusty subdivision with not a single tree in sight? Do you really love the smell of mortar and cement and brick dust that much?'

Now he was being smart and offensive. Mary untied her apron. 'The Cartwrights are moving, I heard.' She had heard, and from Betty Cartwright herself. That nice corner house within walking distance of the Safety Bay school was not even five years old.

Harry scratched his head. Betty and Kevin were always moving. They were behind the hotel at the Malibu Road intersection for just nine months. Then they moved less than a mile up the road. 'The Cartwrights didn't even see a Christmas where they were before.'

'Who wants a Christmas behind a hotel?' Mary took another tactic and poured him a beer, using one of the glasses she had polished three times. 'I'm not saying we should be like Betty's family. But all the nice people are moving down there. It doesn't have the history of a holiday town, that area.'

Harry thought otherwise; he also thought Mary was never happy. Would she tire of him one day? But he sat comfortably at the kitchen table. 'We can go have a look if you like, Marigold. If it'll make you happy, my little flower.' He thought of Kevin Cartwright's big garage and workshop. He could do with a place like that.

She beamed. Of *course* it would make her happy to have a newer home, from where Michael could walk to school. Two of his friends' families were building around Charthouse Road. There was talk of a new line of shops. She could see herself walking down swinging a nice wicker basket.

'There's a reserve down there.'

Harry thought you probably couldn't see the reserve for building sites, but he stayed silent and drank his beer.

'Which means we could get Michael that bike he wants.'

Did she think he was made of money? *'Mary!'*

'And a dog.'

***

Rose and Robbie Coniglio drove up to the yacht club and parked on the verge outside.

She drew her new blue coat around her shoulders and grumbled once more. 'Why they have to have an anniversary celebration in the middle of winter is entirely beyond me, Robbie.'

'Twenty-one years, Rose. Any excuse for a ... Come on, you enjoy a party as much as all of us.'

'I enjoy a party ...' She rose from the passenger seat when Robbie opened her door. She insisted on the car door being opened for her. '... if it's held on some shady veranda or terrace in summer, well after Christmas, with a good barbecue, and lots of salads, and ...'

'We'll have champagne today, love. C'mon. C'mon, Rosie ... and they'll surely have some nice seafood. Maybe a really nice ... what do you call it ...?'

'Chowder, Robbie. Chowder. The twenty-first anniversary of the Cruising Yacht Club in Rockingham cannot fail to give us *chowder*.' Her stinging sarcasm took the smile off his face. 'You think everything's *nice*.'

Rose was turning into her mother, and she wasn't yet twenty-six. They had married very young. Her mother insisted on it when they had gone out for more than six months.

'Has he proposed yet?' That was the question on Rose's mother's red lips every night she returned—on time—from an outing. Mrs Martin refused to call them dates. It was a vulgar word. The whole world was turning into America.

Oh, how many years ago was that? Robbie Coniglio thought back to when he dated Rose, to the envy of her sister, Poppy. Well, he thought those strange looks she gave them were envy.

Now, his business was doing well. Starting a motor servicing place up Kwinana way was a brainwave that went as well as the cars they worked on. His Italian father had passed down know-how and instinctive wisdom, and his canny mother, hands always occupied with tomato sauce and pasta and olive oil and basil had all the acumen of anyone raised around Eighty Road.

Handing his wife a glass of champagne as she was greeted by all their friends, distracted from the disgruntled mood of not five minutes before, he reminisced in silence while his mates chattered about the football and one member's new boat.

Marrying Rose Martin was just another step up. They had no idea, watching all those films at the Melody Drive-In in his big brother's car, that he and Rose would have four children by the time he was twenty-five. The twins were a handful, arriving in the middle as they did, but those girls had all the energy and beauty that mixed heritage could bring.

That night, Aunty Poppy was looking after all four children at their Warnbro house, built to overlook the Sound and the windblown beaches. Rose had asked for them all to be in bed by nine, but they all knew she would let them stay up to watch *Hey Hey It's Saturday*, probably right to its end. Well, perhaps they'd sleep in on Sunday morning.

The house was quiet when they arrived a bit after midnight.

'I told you not to have that last champagne, Rose.' Robbie opened her car door and she weaved slowly through the garage and up the stairs.

'Please, please don't fuss, Robbie. It's not me who's turning into my mother, God rest her restless soul ...' She slurred all her esses, making her husband sigh. 'It's you, Roberto Coniglio. It's you who's turning into a Mrs Martin. All you need is some 'Carnaby Crimson' lipstick!'

He stood at the foot of the staircase and watched her take over from her sister Poppy, who was still knitting in front of the flickering television set.

***

Poppy didn't like Robbie Coniglio. She didn't like Harry Maslin. Poppy would look at all the gangly hormonal adolescents down by the jetty when she was sixteen and pull a secret face at the thought of the future. Everyone believed she should go out with and marry one of them. Not even if they asked on their knees, and she knew no one would. She was a bit too scary to approach.

Marriage was a presumption she tried to clear her mother's mind of, but to no avail.

'Mary's seeing that nice Maslin boy.' Her mother would hint, standing on the back veranda with a cigarette held in two upright fingers. The girls were not allowed to smoke. Oh no. But since Peter Martin had an untimely massive stroke and left her to raise the girls on her own, she took a position at the Rockingham

Hotel, and everyone smoked there. Whenever she mentioned her work, she would annex it with, 'In the *office*, mind!'

'Rose is seeing that ... Rob? Bob? I can't say their name, but they're the Italians round the corner from the bakery.'

'I know, Mum. Everybody knows.'

'Put on something pretty, Poppy. You look so good in blue. Put on a little lipstick.'

'Yes. Why not? Carnaby Crimson.' The twist on her mouth was hilarious, if her mother would only notice.

'What's wrong with ... I've worn it for years!'

'I know, Mum.'

'Before you know it, your sisters will be married with children. Put on something pretty, and ... look, you'll be left behind, Poppy.'

'On the *shelf*, oooh!'

'You won't be joking or smirking when your sisters have families.'

They did have families. And in her heart, she did joke and smirk.

Poppy came back to the Fisher Street house from the draughty place in Singleton, and stayed on well after Mrs Martin died. No one knew what she did with her time, but she worked at the shire council, doing licensing and permits or whatever they did in the brand spanking new offices on Council Avenue.

'And when our population hits thirty thousand,' she could be heard saying to some resident or other, 'we'll qualify to be a city. A city, mind!' Oh dear, was she starting to sound like her mother? Never.

From the first week after she was in that house alone—the house where she and her sisters grew up—she cleared out all the things she hated. Two vans from Vinnies rolled up and took almost everything away.

Standing with arms akimbo, she surveyed the spaces and planned renovations. In six months, the place was unrecognisable. Its corner aspect added to the fresh look it acquired when the front and side were landscaped. Poppy spent a lot of money, but her house was the envy of all the neighbourhood. 'Soon,' she told her reflection in the rippled water bowl of the fountain near the gate, 'soon, everyone will follow suit, and the street will improve.'

Aunty Poppy stayed single. And not for lack of requests to parties and barbecues and trips to Rottnest. She enjoyed all the events she went to, even the Spring Festival, when she emerged onto the foreshore with thousands of others to celebrate the season. She was no wallflower, she joked, as a pun on her name. Everyone laughed, but they knew Poppy was not the marrying kind.

'I could make you happy, Poppy Martin,' Tommy Burton said to her at the tavern one after-work Friday night with other council workers.

She turned and eyed him, about twice as sober as he was. 'Really think so, Tom?' She had a brilliant house, a good job, a holiday every second year, and no one to contradict or betray her. And he thought he could make her happy.

'Reckon I could,' was his lame reply.

She made sure it didn't even go as far as having another Friday drink.

Both her sisters got used to how things were with Poppy, regarding her with a measure of admiration. Somehow or other, she had avoided all the trappings, mess and worry of married life.

'But think of the loneliness,' Rose said to Mary one bright afternoon when all the children were having a good time on the sand at Shoalwater Beach. Their combined picnic was something to behold, and just as delicious, in their differently-coloured Tupperware containers.

Mary poo-poohed and pulled a face. *'Loneliness!* Does our Poppy look sad and lonely to you?'

***

They sat around a table at one of the cafés on the Rockingham Foreshore, two women with oversized handbags and large sunglasses, and one in jeans and a bum-bag.

'So everyone's computers survived all right?'

'We had a guy come down from the city to make sure,' Poppy laughed. 'All that Y2K fuss for nothing. City of Rockingham council lived to work another day! The world did not end.'

'Do you remember when we spoke of this day?'

'What? Which day?'

'Today?'

Mary—called Marigold now, by her new husband—and Rose looked mystified. Their catch-ups were rare, but they all enjoyed them.

Poppy turned and pointed. 'Remember the old jetty? Remember how we sat on it once and thought how we'd be in our late forties when the new millennium arrived?'

'I don't remember. Was I there?' Rose adjusted her sunglasses, hoping she didn't look like she was pushing fifty, hoping she looked just as young as Poppy, who never seemed to change.

Mary, whose silhouette was no longer svelte or reedy, shifted in her chair. 'We never thought of the future in those days. And we'd better drink up because Jeremy is swinging round to drive me back home.'

'All the way up to Scarborough. Whatever possessed you? It's another planet up there.'

Mary looked offended. 'It's much nicer than you think, and Jeremy's from up there, so ...'

'Robbie and I will never move,' Rose said. 'He's too married to his boats and fishing, and ...'

'And the rivalry between those clubs!'

They all laughed.

'What about you, Poppy? You'll never move, surely.'

'The new millennium is treating me and Rockingham just fine.' She didn't say a word about her close friend Barbara, who was also forty-nine, and with whom she was planning a holiday in Austria that Christmas. 'Just fine.'

'Oh, my goodness me. The three flowers!' A loud voice boomed somewhere behind them.

They all looked up and around at a man, silhouetted against the bright light. 'We used to call you that, you know. The three Rocky flowers,' he laughed.

'And who might you be?'

'Ah, just one of the youngsters, the hangers-on, who'd moon over you, whenever you came down to the jetty. Those were the days, eh?'

Marigold was glad she was still recognisable at forty-nine. Rose thought he had a nerve, coming up to them just like that. And Poppy hoped he'd go away as quickly as he appeared. She looked at them. Three flowers, indeed.

**

Free Spirit

Kathy Flint

'Mike! Hey, Mike, over here!' Fiona yelled, jumping up and down.

It took Mike a second to figure out which direction the voice was coming from. He looked over heads to the dock crowded with people. It didn't help having to squint into the bright sun, even when he managed to zero in on the general area; it took a raised hand gesturing him over to pick Fiona out.

'You made it!' Mike threw his arms around her in a suffocating hug. 'Thank you for coming for me.'

'Always happy to help out a friend.' Fiona's eyes flicked up and down at Mike, standing there in his Royal Australian Naval uniform. She'd been asked by her friend Jackie to collect Mike off his ship and take care of him for a week while Jackie was away in Canberra. Fiona agreed, figuring it would be an easy assignment. However, it was a bonus discovering how much Mike was a pleasure on the eyes these days.

As an eleven-year-old, Fiona had fallen under the spell of the ocean when her family moved to Rockingham. There's a romance in the seaside lifestyle. Everyone longs to venture out to the wide blue sea, challenge themselves in new ways and find new water adventures. The combination of fresh sea air and water was irresistible to her, from Naval seamen in white uniforms to sailors on huge yachts to fishermen and recreational boaters.

She stood for a moment, feeling Mike's warm, muscled body against hers, and the smell of his crisp, clean, citrus deodorant.

He kissed her on her cheek before taking a step back and looking her over. 'You haven't changed one bit.'

'You have. You stand head and shoulders above everyone else now. When did you become so tall?' Mike was Jackie's little brother; Jackie was her best friend from high school. As such, he was four years younger than Fiona.

'It's all that wholesome sea air and good naval food.' He laughed.

Mike's hair was still as short and neat as she remembered it from graduation. But now, he was darkly tanned, making his eyes seem startlingly bright. 'You look good.'

'Everyone looks good in uniform.'

'True.' Fiona nodded. 'But have you been working out?'

'No need for gyms on the ship, just months at sea, doing hard, physical labour. Still, hard work never hurt anybody.' He winked at her.

Fiona smiled. They were surrounded by Mike's fellow seamen, their friends and family welcoming them home. She looked over Mike's shoulder at the *HMAS Esperance*. 'Do I get to see this ship I've been hearing about?'

Mike made a weird face. 'I'm afraid I can't take you on board as you're a civilian.'

'That's disappointing.'

'But there's going to be open-to-the-public sessions on the weekend.'

'Will you take me on board then and show me around?'

'Sure. You can be my special guest.'

'It's a date. Come on, let's get you into the car.' Fiona paced off towards where she'd parked her grey Corolla. 'I thought you could stay with me, seeing your sister is away. Okay?'

'Absolutely. It's bad timing, Jackie being away in Canberra for the whole week I'm home. Unfortunately, the Navy doesn't let us have any input into their schedules. I haven't seen Jackie since we caught up in Sydney six months ago.'

'I'll be your tour guide, if you want?'

'I know my way around, Fiona. I hope Rockingham hasn't changed that much.' Mike looked around from side to side at the spectacular view as she drove her car over the high, narrow causeway bridge. Leaving the naval base, they headed towards the mainland. To the left, Palm Beach and the town of Rockingham sat on the edge of Cockburn Sound, the water as placid as bathwater, and to the right, Point Peron curved out into the deep blue seawater of the Indian Ocean. A cool breeze swept through the car; it smelled fresh and briny. He smiled, leaned over and patted her left knee.

'You okay there?' she asked. 'My car's small for the size of you.'

He grinned. 'I'm not complaining. It's good of you to collect me.'

'My pleasure.'

'I do appreciate you stepping up to look after me while I'm here in port.'

'Just like old times. If I remember rightly, you used to tag along with Jackie and me whenever we went fishing or exploring Point Peron.'

'Mum was happy to have me out of the house, however, Jackie wasn't always pleased, especially when you two became interested in boys. Jackie always tried to lose me or send me away to the shop to buy a lolly.'

Fiona laughed. 'Yes, she did, but you have to admit you were a whiny kid when you were about ten.'

***

Once they reached Fiona's home in Safety Bay, she parked the car and stepped through the front door with Mike following. She dropped her keys into a bowl on the kitchen counter.

'Do you want me to show you around my place, or do you remember where everything is?'

'How about you show me where I'm going to sleep, so I can drop off my stuff?'

Fiona pointed along the corridor. 'The guest room is at the end of the hallway. And you have your own ensuite, for privacy.'

Mike smiled widely. 'Bliss. I haven't had any privacy on that ship. No such thing there.'

'Anytime you need privacy, say so and I'll make myself scarce.'

Mike scrunched up his nose and made a face. 'Not from you, silly. It's just not as easy as you think to live with all those other guys in such cramped quarters for months on end.' Mike bent over and gave Fiona a peck on her cheek as he picked up his duffle bag and walked down the hallway.

'Make yourself at home. When you're ready, I'll be on the back patio. I'll find us some drinks.'

As she waited for him to join her, Fiona wondered. Would it be such a scandal for her to have a romantic attachment with Mike? She didn't want to upset Jackie, as they had been friends since school days, but other than her, who cared what other people thought? She had known Mike just as long as Jackie, they had the same group of school friends, they knew each other well, and their families had history together. Wasn't that the best basis for romance anyone could hope for?

Fifteen minutes later, Mike found her out the back, wine in hand, sitting staring at the ocean. 'Hope you don't mind; I took a shower to freshen up and change out of my uniform.'

She eyed him up and down, taking in the tight grey T-shirt stretched across his broad chest and the denim shorts which accentuated his tanned thighs of steel. 'All good?'

'Yes, fine.'

'Would you like to join me in a wine or would you prefer a beer?'

'Beer, please. I'm not much of a wine drinker.'

She leapt up and grabbed a cold can of beer from her bar fridge.

They sat talking while the sunset turned into night, remembering those carefree days before the Navy took Mike away—swimming all summer as a group of high school kids by the jetty, cooking fresh-caught fish over open fires on the beach at Point Peron and playing football at the oval. Fiona had been a champion goal kicker in school sports. However, when they graduated from high school, it had all changed.

'I expected everyone to stay around locally, but it seemed everybody took off for jobs or careers over on the East Coast. I haven't seen anyone from school since then,' Fiona complained. 'Even Jackie and I only seem to catch up over the phone lately. We have fun whenever we do manage to get together, but that's not too often these days.'

They sat there, sharing news, updates and gossip, talking, drinking and staring out at the stars in the sky.

***

Next morning at breakfast, they discussed what Fiona had planned for the day.

'I don't know anything about sailing.' Mike shrugged.

'But you're a sailor. How can you not know about sailing?' Fiona shook her head.

'Sailing is a pleasure activity, and quite different from being in the Navy. On the ship, it's all about working the eight-hour shifts, swabbing the decks, maintaining the steel structures, then eating in the galley and sleeping with the other men.'

'We have to put all this free time of yours to good use.' Fiona waved a dismissive hand. 'So, we're going to the yacht club this morning, and I'll teach you everything you need to know. It's not hard. I taught my cousin to sail, and he's younger than you.'

Mike shook his head. 'How can I say no?'

'You can't and that's it.' Fiona rose and cleared the table.

When they drove to the Safety Bay Yacht Club, Mike could see a dozen sailboats bobbing in a calm body of turquoise water, protected from the waves of the Indian Ocean by a rocky island. The boats looked all the same—white fibreglass hulls, aluminium masts, sails shrouded in dark blue or brown canvas. 'Which is ours?'

Fiona pointed to the yacht moored on the far right. 'That's ours. It's Dad's boat. He named it *Free Spirit.*'

'She's beautiful.'

Fiona waved to a young lad standing next to a beached rubber dinghy, a tall, slender, dark-haired guy, still in his teen years, his face covered in acne. Fiona made introductions, 'Mike, this is Kirk, my cousin. And Kirk, this is Mike, my friend Jackie's brother.'

They shook hands. Kirk stood taller than Mike, and they both made Fiona feel short. She organised Kirk to take them out to the yacht. Turning to Mike, she said, 'Load the gear, he'll ferry us out.' The outboard engine sputtered as they crossed the water.

Up close, *Free Spirit* was far bigger than Mike had expected. The canvas sail covers and cockpit enclosure were all sun-bleached. The teak trim looked weathered, and rust flecked the chrome brightwork. Mike clucked his tongue and shook his head. 'Needs some serious maintenance done on this one.'

'True. Dad's let it go. He's been too busy at work.'

As they scrambled on board the yacht, Fiona took control. 'Make yourself at home, Mike. Stow your gear below. There is a queen-sized bed in the forward berth. Throw your stuff there.' As Mike made his way below, Fiona turned to Kirk, 'He's a nice guy, real smart. You'll like him.'

Kirk nodded and added, 'He's a bit young for you, isn't he?'

She didn't need her cousin to highlight the obvious. 'We're just hanging out while Jackie's away in Canberra. Nothing serious.'

'Sure. Whatever.' Then Kirk reported he'd already placed an esky full of drinks and other supplies on the yacht.

She thanked him with a kiss to his cheek and waved as the rubber dinghy chugged away.

The boat's beam was wide at its broadest point, making plenty of space in the galley kitchen, and the dining area had booth seating for four. Storage was plentiful, and all the woodwork was lacquered teak. However, the carpet was worn to the weft in places, and the upholstery had multiple stains and looked the worse for wear.

Moments later, Mike joined Fiona, who sat in the cockpit, shaded by canvas, sipping on a Coke.

'Help yourself.' She pointed to the esky packed with ice and cans of all varieties.

Mike chose a Pepsi and popped the can. Folding his arms and lounging back, he watched the fluffy clouds float across the azure-blue sky while the boat rocked from side to side and waves mumbled against the hull. 'Not bad.'

Fiona grinned. 'I thought this would be fun for you.'

'It still might be.' Mike took a swig from his can.

'You're in good shape; sailing should come easy to you.' She realised she was flirting with him but couldn't help herself as she batted her eyelids. He's one hot-looking guy. Why shouldn't she? No harm done.

A light breeze began to blow across their bow, the water sparkled, and the boom creaked.

Fiona jumped up, held onto the large wheel and barked orders. 'Here comes the Fremantle Doctor. Pull up the anchor, Mike. Hoist the mainsail. Unfurl the gib. Loosen the winches. Where's the winch handle? Watch your head on the boom.'

Fiona did most of the talking, instructing him, and Mike found himself being more charmed as each hour passed. He loved the sound of her voice and the way she gestured with her hands as she spoke. She was self-assured and purposeful.

Mike focused on Fiona, watching her manoeuvre the yacht, yanking on ropes, swinging the sail over their heads, the material catching the strong ocean breeze before sending them speeding through the water. All the while, he sat there transfixed. He'd never seen a woman like Fiona before. It was as if she was somehow attached to the yacht. She seemed to know every inch of the yacht, every creak and groan, knew what to shift and pull and push on a split second before it needed to be done; all while the sea tossed around them, spraying both of them in a salty mist.

Unfortunately, the good weather didn't hold. The dark grey clouds rolled in from the north, and the sky went dark and broody before they knew it.

'Hold on!' she hollered over to him, as her hair whipped around in the wind. The sky cracked open, and a flood came pouring down, both of them drenched in an instant. The mainsail caught a gust of wind and took the yacht into a wall of water, the boat groaning. Still Fiona steered her, trying as best she could to keep her steady, her face locked into a grimace, her body tensed, her eyes burning bright. 'Untie the front gib!' she shouted, her voice barely breaking through the din of the sudden storm.

Mike hopped up and almost fell overboard, the boat pitching this way and that. He grabbed the wooden handrail and held tight as he made his way forward to the winch. He untied the ropes and watched as the sail furled smaller and smaller. The boat at last slowed, riding the waves instead of crashing headlong into them.

'Now what?' Mike shouted.

Fiona stared at the sky, hands like a vice on the wheel, a vein throbbing in her neck as her mane of blonde hair flew to the side. 'I think we should turn about and head for home.' And she laughed, the rain flicking off her face.

Mike made his way back to the cockpit and grabbed onto the wheel, standing side by side with her as the rain continued to come down in buckets. Mike helped Fiona turn the wheel as she steered it in a one-hundred-and-eighty-degree turn, the boom and mainsail crashing over their heads as they went about in the strong gale. The two of them stood, feet rooted to the deck, hands locked onto the wheel, side by side, wave after wave hitting them as the sky went from grey to black and back again. They'd never felt so damned cold and soaked through. Half an hour later, the last miserable drop hit the top of the cockpit.

Fiona's smile grew bigger. 'Made it. All good. That was fun.'

Mike stood back against the railing, looking at her with a crooked grin. 'I wouldn't call that fun, but I'm glad we made it, safe and sound.' He looked out at the ocean, the waves at last barely breaking, and he finally exhaled. 'Seemed like I held my breath all that time.'

'You weren't afraid we wouldn't make it, were you?' Fiona stared at Mike, his smile ever present.

'No, of course not. I'm a naval man. I know what the sea can throw at us. However, your ship is a wee bit smaller than what I'm used to.'

They both laughed.

Fiona added, 'At least you know you're alive.'

'I'm glad I'm *still* alive,' Mike said. 'But you're shivering, Fiona. Let me warm you.' He closed the gap between them, as he wrapped his thick arms around her, his hands rubbed up and down her back and shoulders. They stood there for some time, getting gently rocked back and forth, until his body warmed her a few degrees and her quaking finally stopped.

She looked at him, lost in those deep green eyes, and it seemed like a good idea to give him a kiss, right there and then.

'Wow! Nice.' He pulled her in closer for another kiss, deeper, longer and more passionate than the first.

The sun broke through the clouds. They stood silently in sunlight as they sailed the yacht back to its mooring spot.

***

As soon as they were back at home, Fiona locked the door. Once inside, Mike pushed her back against the door and kissed her again. His kiss was deep, penetrating, breath-stealing, and it filled her with desire.

She grinned as he stepped back and ripped off his shirt. His broad shoulders and thick chest tapered to a flat stomach and narrow waist. She licked her lips, wanting to kiss him all over.

Unbuttoning her shirt, his fingers fumbled around on her chest.

He was too young, and her best friend's brother, two good reasons to not get involved with him. Fiona knew she shouldn't be going into these dangerous and uncharted waters, but it excited her to be so reckless.

He whispered about how they were made for each other, how he had loved her since he was twelve years old, how his love for her would overcome all obstacles.

Brushing her hair away, he kissed the base of her neck. She leaned against him, comfortable in his arms. She wondered if she was in over her depth this time.

It was going to be a passionate week of endless opportunities.

Heritage Building Classroom

Nada Lubay

In 1935, Rockingham Beach Primary School officially opened its doors. The first settlers constructed a standard-design school building using locally sourced timber. This small, one-room wooden classroom dates back to the pre-Second World War era. Ideally located near shops, the post office, and the beach, it is well suited to accommodate the growing population.

However, the town faced setbacks during the war. Young men left to join the army, causing a shortage of builders, labour, and materials. This halted the additional building plans until 1946.

After the war, at the opening ceremony, families of the first settlers from the district and the local MP gathered to celebrate this special occasion. The scene was alive with excitement; the air filled with a buzz of anticipation. Children's laughter and chatter echoed through the surroundings, adding to the lively atmosphere. As local dignitaries planted trees, the earthy smell of freshly turned soil wafted through the air, creating a sense of new beginnings. The small, tight-knit community was brimming with enthusiasm, eager for the construction of teachers' quarters to attract educators to move from the city to their beautiful coastal town.

Rockingham Beach Primary School still stands proudly on Bay View Street, the historic grounds where early settlers built their first timber classroom. Due to its historical significance, this wooden classroom is heritage-listed. As you approach the old building, the scent of aged wood fills the air, blending with the rich, earthy aroma of the surrounding trees. The structure serves as a reminder of the past, and its simple timber frame tells a historical story. Inside, the sounds of children's laughter resonate, harmonising with the whispers of the falling leaves outside.

With time passing, the school remains committed to providing quality education through ongoing renovations and the addition of portable classrooms. This commitment reflects its resilience and enduring legacy. Rockingham Beach Primary Campus is an independent public school that collaborates with the Education Support Centre to foster inclusive learning environments for students with special needs. All students receive support to excel academically, socially, and personally. The teaching team is committed to ensuring positive outcomes for every student. One of the school's exceptional features is its nurturing environment, which values each child.

***

In 1980, Rockingham was a small country town where our five-year-old son attended Rockingham Beach Primary pre-school. We chose that school due to its proximity to our new home and its reputation for maintaining traditional and academically rigorous educational values.

Over time, Rockingham has developed into a large and prosperous city. As the town experienced a population boom, the school expanded its facilities by adding more classrooms to accommodate the growing number of students. Modern buildings appeared alongside historic architecture, creating a vibrant atmosphere on campus. The newly refurbished classrooms highlight the unique blend of old and new while preserving the ancient trees that have stood for generations.

***

In 2016, the second generation of our family enrolled in preschool, and we were thrilled to see our granddaughter starting this new chapter. Watching her tiny shoes and tearful goodbyes while surrounded by the sounds of eager chatter and sniffles was a memorable experience. The feeling of déjà vu reminded us that she was now sitting in the same classroom her father had attended forty years ago. Although the old wooden desks had been replaced with modern furniture, the faded paint on the ceiling still reflected the school's long history.

Throughout those years, I dedicated time to volunteering at various school events, including PC meetings, discos, and countless sausage sizzles. As a member of the school board, I had the opportunity to interact with friendly teachers, staff, and enthusiastic students. This experience allowed me to witness firsthand that the school's spirit is still vibrant and alive.

In 2020, the school planned to celebrate its 125th anniversary, and the event organisers busily prepared for a celebration of the historic building. This occasion was particularly special, and everyone was eager to participate in the preparations. Teachers and students organised a fun event that included games, speeches, delicious food, and music. Excitement buzzed throughout the school as everyone looked forward to honouring the town's first settlers. A traditional tea party, featuring scones, local marmalade, and cream, was enjoyed by students and teachers dressed in colonial attire.

Students created a variety of arts and crafts for display alongside culturally significant Indigenous paintings. The atmosphere was filled with excitement as people visualised the celebration, the old walls echoing with history and a new generation gathering in the shade of a large gum tree, its leaves rustling in the afternoon sea breeze.

Unfortunately, the celebrations were cancelled due to the global COVID-19 pandemic and the unforeseen circumstances of lockdowns, which disappointed both students and teachers. During the lockdown, the old structure stood in eerie silence. Its timeworn wooden frame creaked under the weight of the years, with every crack and crevice seemingly whispering stories of the past. The air was thick with the musty odour of accumulated dust and decay, and a heavy, sweet smell lingered like a forgotten dream. History resonated within the rough-hewn timbers, where the scent and faint echoes of laughter and sorrow felt almost tangible.

**

Rockingham Beach Primary School is now a modern facility, yet it retains elements of its original design. The old, weathered timber classroom still stands proudly as a testament to skilled artisanship. In today's modern world, the old building is used for after-school services and special occasions, such as art exhibitions and students' arts and crafts activities. During recess, children can be seen playing happily, while others sit in the shade of a large gum tree that was planted by the first settlers. Observing these joyful moments evokes a sense of nostalgia.

**

In 2024, Rockingham Beach Primary School hosted the Year 6 graduation ceremony. It was a proud moment filled with laughter and happy tears as we celebrated our granddaughter's achievements. Many parents, grandparents, visitors, and the local MP attended the event, creating a delightful atmosphere as everyone acknowledged the school's growth and prosperity.

Rockingham Beach School has demonstrated the values and traditions of the first settlers. The school is committed to providing a good education, strong pastoral care, and encouraging community involvement. The only significant change over the years has been the integration of modern technology, which has been embraced by a younger generation of tech-savvy students and their families.

Home Sweet Home

Nada Lubay

We moved to Western Australia in 1980 with just one suitcase and little else, a significant milestone for a young married couple and their child. We purchased a one-way ticket on the famous Indian Pacific train to escape the rainy weather in Adelaide and start a new life in sunny Perth.

During our long journey across the Nullarbor Plain, our five-year-old son was entertained by watching kangaroos hop across the red desert. The rhythmic clacking of the train and the scent of diesel soothed our young child, helping him fall asleep. The flat landscape seemed to stretch endlessly, featuring a treeless and barren desert extending from southern Australia to the Western Australian border. However, the breathtaking sunsets transformed the scene, illuminating the dusty red terrain and creating the illusion that the earth and sky were merging into one.

Upon arriving at Perth Station the following morning, we were greeted by our friends who had moved to Western Australia a few years earlier in search of new fortune in the booming mining industry. Witnessing their prosperous lifestyles and spacious family homes filled us with hope that this new place would provide us with a bright future.

We soon discovered that Perth is the most isolated city in the southern hemisphere. In 1962, astronaut John Glenn named Perth 'The City of Lights' during his orbit around Earth while he communicated with NASA via a satellite connection in the Australian outback. While orbiting in space, he saw the lights of Perth shining brightly against the vast darkness of the Indian Ocean below and the equally dark Australian outback ahead. He remarked, '*The lights show up very well; please thank everybody for turning them on.*'

The next day, our friends drove us along a scenic route highlighting Perth's stunning beaches. We visited Kings Park, where we enjoyed the breathtaking views of the landscape and the Swan River below, harmoniously contrasting with the modern skyscrapers of Perth's architecture.

A week later, we rented a car and took a scenic tour of the south. The drive through the Margaret River vineyard region was breathtaking, with the salty ocean breeze and crashing waves surrounding us.

We took a moment to appreciate the area's beauty, admiring the colonial buildings decorated with vibrant colours, and the inviting aroma of freshly brewed dark-roast coffee drifting from local cafés further enhanced the lively atmosphere. After enjoying the stunning natural scenery, we continued our journey past the giant trees in Pemberton, ultimately reaching Australia's southernmost point.

On our way back to Perth, we stopped in Rockingham, a small town that, due to its proximity to the bustling city of Fremantle, only added to its charm. We sat on the beach, enjoying fish and chips wrapped in newspaper while listening to the melodic sounds of seagulls soaring above us. The invigorating scent of the salty sea air captivated our senses. A gentle breeze carried the fresh aroma of the ocean, and the soft sand beneath our feet provided a comforting sensation, reassuring us that this was the perfect place to build our lives.

Seated at the Rockingham foreshore beneath the shade of towering pine trees, we found the tranquillity of the moment truly memorable. The cool grass under our feet reminded us of European landscapes, evoking memories of Alpine meadows. Instead of snow-capped peaks, our gaze fell upon the vast expanse of stunning white sandy beach, stretching endlessly towards Fremantle.

One of the most unforgettable experiences was walking across the exposed sand bars to reach Penguin Island during low tide. It was a unique adventure that would remain etched in our memory forever. The air was filled with the strong scent of the sea, blended with the musky aroma of lazy seals basking in the warm sun. The gentle crashing of the waves created a soothing soundtrack, complemented by the playful clicks and whistles of dolphins as they leapt gracefully through the crystal-clear waters. The beautiful scenery of the natural flora and fauna around us painted a future full of promise, making it an ideal place to raise a young family. A deep sense of calm washed over us as we put down our roots here, confident that it would always be our haven. We quietly affirmed that Rockingham was now our new home.

***

During our first year living in Rockingham, we rented a rundown unit that primarily housed disadvantaged and unemployed individuals. We chose that rundown flat on Thorpe Street, close to Rockingham Beach Primary School, where our son started preschool. Knowing this was just temporary accommodation made it easier to manage our daily struggles.

The dusty two-bedroom unit on the top floor needed a good cleaning, and after buying basic second-hand furniture, we had only enough money left to purchase our first colour TV. It holds a special place in my memories because of the sights and sounds of our small-screen Rank Arena model complete with an indoor antenna that we continually had to adjust to improve the picture quality.

The colour television gleaming under a hefty price tag was such a vast novelty, a humble entertainment for the young family. Nineteen-eighty also held another great significance, mainly due to the Moscow Summer Olympics in Russia. The scenes and sounds of the Olympic Games radiating from the screen transformed our living room into a grand spectacle. This marked the first time in Olympic history that two flag bearers were introduced, symbolising unity and strength. It was exciting to see Australia among the first countries to enter the stadium, proudly carrying the Australian flag. We cheered for the Australian swimming team, jumping enthusiastically during the races and shouting words of encouragement for their successes.

When my husband began working at Western Mining, and I found a job at a local travel agency, our fortunes started to change. We purchased an old car and began saving for a deposit on a block of land within walking distance of the beach, where we planned to build our first dream home.

***

The following year, we moved into our new home. At the entrance, near the doorbell, hung a wooden sign that read, HOME SWEET HOME. We soon began socialising at home again and welcomed many new friends. My husband and his workmates liked to watch Aussie Rules football while the women chatted about their children's school activities.

Our built-in BBQ featured a wood-burning fire, centred on the distinctive aroma of Jarrah wood. The scent of freshly caught crayfish and prawns filled the air, wafting throughout the garden.

Like many of his schoolmates, our son rode his bike to school, and after school, kids played in the park without parents worrying about their safety. All the kids were fascinated by the Star Wars movies, collecting figurines and enjoyed playing a Lightsaber game. On weekends, the kids would watch *Sesame Street* or rent a movie to enjoy on the video recorder. They also played games on early electronic devices, with every child on the street owning a Commodore 64.

After a few years, our backyard blossomed into a lush garden. The front yard featured native plants and untamed bottlebrush bushes that attracted bees and birds, complementing the playground across the road. With its scenic lake, this park attracted a variety of birds. Before sunrise, possums and kangaroos hopped in the park, grazing on the green grass where native plants thrive. On the other side of the park, cockatoos played among the olive trees. These noisy parrots often gathered in groups, shaking the branches as they feasted on ripe olives and skillfully spat out the pips.

When life settled into a work routine, we enjoyed coming home and relaxing in the backyard with a cold beer or a glass of wine. The outdoor patio's lush greenery and decorative hanging baskets highlight a variety of colourful flowers, creating a fantastic atmosphere for entertaining.

Reflecting on 1980, Rockingham was a charming, small country town with a close-knit community and a population of 20,000. Neighbours knew one another and were not concerned about leaving their front doors unlocked. The town had no traffic lights, just a small shopping centre and an old pub. The lack of streetlights contributed to its charm, allowing the stars to shimmer in the night sky like undiscovered jewels.

During weekends, locals gathered at the foreshore for picnics and barbecues. People were amazed as dolphins playfully performed acrobatics in the water while children splashed around and built sandcastles, enjoying the soothing afternoon breeze on their sunburned skin. As the sun set, the horizon glowed with majestic red and orange hues, making it the perfect time to sit on the jetty and enjoy fishing.

Over the past forty-five years of living in Rockingham, we have witnessed its transformation into a popular city. Today, this beautiful seaside town has become a thriving city where everyone wants to live.

Fast forward to 2025, Rockingham's population has increased to 150,000 and continues to grow. The beach is bustling with a vibrant mix of locals and tourists, and by afternoon, restaurants are packed. The New Year fireworks have gained immense popularity, leading people to arrive early in the day to secure the best spots under the pine trees at Rockingham Foreshore. The beach and boardwalk are decorated with colourful Christmas lights, and a live band plays while children gather around Santa, dancing to *Jingle Bells* on stage.

At the end of the summer school holidays, the local park, which features a war memorial, comes alive with vibrant colours. An orchestra performs an open-air symphony under a bright, starry sky. On this peaceful evening, families enjoy picnics, and are captivated by the majestic classical music filling the crisp air illuminated only by stars. My husband and I sat near the stage, watching children joyfully dance in front of it. We were delighted to see our granddaughter and her school friends happily dancing to the melodies of *The Nutcracker.*

While enjoying our picnic and engaging in a lively discussion during the intermission, my husband playfully said,

"We are so lucky to be living in Rockingham; our home is our castle. This is where we belong!"

I turned around, smiling, and replied, "Rockingham is our paradise – now you know, my dear, why I named our house *Home Sweet Home*."

***

In the Beginning

Rosanne Dingli

She traversed the space she could use on the forward deck, reaching the end near the cordoned-off steps. The passengers in steerage grouped mid-ships were not allowed up where she was, and she did not like the close and curious scrutiny of their upturned faces when she emerged from the companionway, so she had to choose her times to venture up and out. She also liked to avoid crew and members of the ship's company, namely the captain and his men, who were often top-side.

The sound of wind through the sails was dreadful, frightening, especially when the canvas flapped and cracked like whips, or whistled and wailed like some demented creature. The other women seemed to quite like it, and took to staying out there, with shawls wrapped around their heads, cheeks rosy in the fresh breeze. There were only three other female passengers left in her class now, and one remarkable man among perhaps thirty others.

He had a similar face to what might be seen in a portrait gallery, such as those she had seen at Somerset House, when on a visit with her aunt. A craggy face, with piercing eyes under greying brows, and a bearded chin that seemed to suggest determination hardened by adversity. Those were what she noticed about him first.

Losing her husband to some unnameable stomach infection, which had killed two women so far, not long after they sailed from London in January, was a blow she could not in a thousand days have foreseen. They were ruined, due to his lack of acumen, and spent their last few pounds on this settlement voyage to parts unknown. They were attracted by the land promised to them, a house, good weather, and numerous other benefits. But they were hardly on board ten days after their last stop in Falmouth, Cornwall, when he expired, groaning out his pain on their narrow bunk. 'Australia,' were his last words. 'Marianne, Marianne ... *Australia*.' What could she do but hold his hand and wait for the ship's doctor to pronounce him dead?

'He's gone, Mrs Ambrose. Gone, I'm afraid.'

They tipped him, bound in a canvas shroud, onto a long board to slide him into the roaring sea as she watched, appalled. Was that how they disposed of those women?

Oh, Francis! He would never see Australia. One kind woman put an arm around her, and another offered a comforting pat on the hand, not attempting to reach her with words in her numb shocked silence. Captain Halliburton read a few stammered lines from a soggy book as she watched that shroud slip and splash into the forever waves, whose spume dampened her hat and flapping shawl and dress hem. 'Oh, Francis. You could never beat bad luck.' She wiped tears of disappointment away with the back of a lace-gloved hand.

'I heard that.' The man with the chiselled face looked down at her trim figure with something like disapproval in his eyes, but how could she tell? In that instant, all she could really feel was fear of facing a voyage alone, of landing in a strange land alone, of starting a new life alone, for her journey was irreversible; she could never return to Whitechapel.

Everyone's words seemed to come and go with the fierce rollers that hit the side of the ship *Rockingham* with all the might of the furious inclement weather. This was never forecast, this nasty rain, this unrelenting wind; but neither was the death of Francis, her ever-loving but incompetent husband, a man she could never bring herself to adore, like her aunt demanded she should. He had a set of inveterate habits. Francis was unlucky at trade, unlucky at cards, and—she had heard once in the haberdashery in Whitechapel—unlucky in his choice of wife. Really? She did her best, but she was never one to laugh off misfortune with a jolly shrug and chuckle.

The tall stranger sought to stand by her side on deck. He was often there, staring out at the waves towards a grey-on-grey horizon, whenever she ventured out on deck. Holding fast to the gunwale, unsteady on her feet, she would wonder where—which of her two places to sit and wait—was more uncomfortable. Below, in the stifling cabin which she now occupied alone, seasickness would take her by the scruff of the neck and the bowl of her belly if she gave one fleeting thought to how she was imprisoned in a tossing, floating wooden cell. On deck, she contemplated dark fathoms of seawater below her, and immense waves that seemed high enough to engulf the *Rockingham*. It petrified her and glued her to the boards in her thin boots.

The first month was agony, the second worse. By the third month, when they were somewhere out so far from land she thought in bewildered weakness she had forgotten what a tree looked like, or a hill, or a field of billowing grass, she found that she had lost the acute sense of departure. Gone was that regretful sensation she deeply felt when the last sight of England was a diminishing blue line on a tipping and tilting horizon. The series of disasters that accompanied and delayed their departure, from sails taken away by a gale, to a lost anchor, to being stranded on Goodwin Sands, was a ghostly memory. What she felt now was a sense of increasing expectation; a sense of impending arrival. It stayed with her a considerable length of time, that longing to sight land. She was starting to look forward, rather than back.

'It won't be long now. Five days, perhaps six, Captain Halliburton says.' It was that man again. Could he sense what she felt?

Would it finally end, that pitching and tossing and putting up with interrupted sleep, bad food, interminable noise, and vile smells? The sense of arrival was big within her, huge, like a swallowed morsel that stuck in her chest, and hurt. She hurt with the need to arrive, so much that she hardly listened to the grey man who made it a point to stand by her side when he emerged from the companionway. He ducked to avoid swinging ropes, stepped over things rolling wetly on the deck, placed legs far apart and swung from the knees in time with the waves. 'We won't know ourselves when we land. We'll not be able to balance on solid, stable ground.' It sounded very nearly like an educated voice, the voice of one who normally would have no place on a voyage of that nature. Why was he sailing out to resettle?

All she did was nod to his sentences. He called her *missus*, which she resented, because she did have a name. But the man who gave her that name lay 'full fathom five', as her aunt might quote, under the waves out from England. What on earth was she to do on arrival?

'Obey instructions at the settlement,' she was told. Land had been granted, building was under way, they said.

A bad storm—a frighteningly violent tempest—struck just after land was sighted. Just as someone shouted behind her, and then all on deck at once.

'Australia!'

Someone said the date aloud on deck. She heard it as she ran for the companionway in a sharp drive of what felt like hail. The wind was tremendous, the lightning and thunder like nothing she ever witnessed; forks of fire shooting into the ocean. Once down the steps, and close to the passage where her cabin was, the man appeared, looking like a drenched ghoul in the half-dark.

'It's bad, missus. Very bad. If I were a religious man, I'd be on my knees now.'

She never said much to him, but this warranted a response. 'God looks after us, whether we are religious or not.' Or so her aunt had told her. 'Perhaps we should all be on ...'

There was a terrific jarring jolt. It cut Marianne Ambrose's sentence in half and threw her bodily towards him. He fell backward, with her on top of him. The sound of splitting, crushing, shattering timber was all about them, and then screams and yells from all sides.

She felt someone help her up, and the man scrambled to his feet, holding his left arm and growling softly. 'Argh. Ah—the last thing one wants at this stage. An injury.' He looked towards her, being helped by a female passenger to right herself and see to rearranging her clothing.

'I'm not hurt. No, no—I am quite all right,' she had to insist to all who crowded around.

The sound of shouts and panicked screaming abated, children's shrieks still deafening. People moved away, and the rush of terror lost its power. There were another few jolts and jerks as the vessel settled, which pushed everyone this way and that.

'We have run aground, missus.'

It took her a second to understand what his words could mean.

'The *Rockingham* has run aground. The keel has met a reef, and we've settled on the bottom.' With that the man, cradling his arm, leaving his hat on the floor where it fell, hurried past her and ascended to the upper deck.

'The *bottom!*' Her fear of deep water rose in her gullet.

To her horror, they were to spend the night on board.

***

What stuck in Marianne's head as she sat at one of the long tables for breakfast below deck was the date someone sang out in the aftermath of the violent grounding. 'May fourteen! The fourteenth of May!' Everything was slightly askew, but they had been asked to keep order, calm and quiet. Most complied, even if everything was tilted to one side. It was just possible for a plate of bread and butter to rest on the table without sliding away, and a saucer-less cup if held in a hand would sooth and nourish. They had to make sure no one went hungry. Hungry passengers were a sure promise of chaos and rebellion, the captain knew that.

The grey man found a seat across from her, and lay a hand on the table to attract her attention.

'How is your arm?' She knew to be polite. Discourtesy never solved predicaments. And she sensed they were in some difficulty.

He nodded to dismiss her question and flexed his elbow to show it was moving well. 'Let me tell you my name, and then I beg you to listen to ...' He looked around, indicating that what he had to say was not for everyone's ears. 'I am Bill Ledgard. Let this serve as our formal introduction, if you please, missus.'

Sensing that this was to prove important, Marianne nodded, stood, left her plate and cup with the woman next to her, and started for the deck.

'I am Mrs Francis Ambrose. I'm Marianne Ambrose,' she said, looking at his shoes and hers, which faced each other on the ship's boards, sodden with rain and spume.

'Listen, now. The only way a woman on her own will survive this is with the help of a man. I watched a rowing boat go out at dawn. It was swept away by enormous waves. No one died, but it was a trial, an exhausting test of nerve and limb, Mrs Ambrose.' He paused and sniffed.

'Go on.'

'They're taking all the women with families. God knows there are enough children on this vessel. They're rowing them in to the beach.'

She nodded. The entire voyage was accompanied by children's screams, yelps, cries, laughter and tears.

'They're keeping the bachelors back.'

'Oh.'

'Might I give you a plan, missus?'

She looked up into grey eyes lit by a kind of inner fire.

'Mrs Ambrose—may I?'

She nodded once more.

He took a mighty breath. 'You are to tell Captain Halliburton that you and I are together. He will only believe it coming from you. He will put us into the same boat, and in that way I'll ... ah ... do my best to protect you. If we capsize ...'

Marianne Ambrose gasped.

'... then I shall save you, being a strong swimmer. Because, missus, he is insisting we continue to disembark even in this bad weather. He thinks the ship is breaking up.'

'I ... oh dear. I'm alone, Mr Ledgard. And I cannot ...'

'You will be with me.'

She said her hopeful words to the captain in between a thousand other requests, entreaties, demands shouted at him by a thousand other mouths babbling around her.

'Yes, yes,' the man said. 'Good, good. Same boat as Bill Ledgard. Yes.'

Other people's shouts and calls dismissed her, and she was once more by the big man's side. 'Now get your belongings together. These are mine.' He pointed to a small trunk by his foot.

By the time she returned on deck with her box and bag, he was sidling what looked like a handful of coin to a sailor, and before she knew it, they were side by side on a boat rowed by four strong men. Perhaps another dozen souls sat around them, and their cries of dismay were in her ears when the current swept them out the minute the boat was lowered to the waves. Out to sea they drifted, out and further out, until the *Rockingham* was a smudge in the distance, and the land a blur.

Just as suddenly, the current wheeled and churned, and returned them to the ship, pushed by several awful waves. The surf was cruel, but with some strong rowing they were closer to the beach in under fifteen minutes. All around the boat floated sundry soaked wet belongings, foaming in the surf. Boxes and crates, bags, packages and chests. Hats, jackets, shoes, books and children's toys drifted towards them and away, some drifting out, other bits and pieces in, and much of it sinking to the sandy bottom.

Marianne held a hand to her mouth, but returned it quickly to hold on to the gunwale, not a moment too soon, because the boat tilted harshly to Bill Ledgard's side and he was swept into the water.

'Oh no! Oh no!' There was absolutely nothing she could do but cling to her seat for dear life. His wooden trunk floated off, and so did her leather bag.

But the man swam and suddenly stood in the surf, with waves crashing onto his back. He was knocked over and stood again, waved a signal, picked up the trunk that swashed past, and started to wade in with it on his shoulder, helping an older man to his feet as he came, and then a youth, and then a woman who had fallen bodily into the water.

When the boat crunched on the beach, Marianne breathed again, tumbled out, found her box and trudged up to the waterline, her skirts drenched and dragging behind her.

It was another good half-hour before they both stood on the dunes, with what was left of their things at their feet. They looked out to sea.

'What do you think will happen to the *Rockingham*?' she asked. 'Look at it. It doesn't look good for much.'

Bill Ledgard reached for his trunk. What was fire in his eyes before looked now like relief. 'I neither know nor care. It's brought us here, hasn't it? Being with you got me off that godforsaken vessel. It *will* break up.'

Her eyes widened in surprise at his changed attitude. 'I suppose. Now we must await instructions, mustn't we? They promised land. Houses, they said. They said they would call our settlement Clarence. I wonder if ...'

'They promised you the moon, and will give you sixpence.' He picked up his chest. 'I won't wait for that.'

'Oh! We must. Instructions will ...'

'Not me, missus. Not me. You wait *for instructions* if you so please. I'm heading north to the mouth of a river I was told holds a free settlement ... called Fremantle.' He promptly turned in the grassy dune and swiped a hand to his forehead as a cursory leave-taking.

Mrs Marianne Ambrose mutely watched him slip and slide away in sand and tall grass until his feet hit stable ground. He never turned to look her way, and she never saw him again.

***

Bryan, C P, writing as Cygnet, *The Rockingham, 1830*, Number 9 in a series of booklets about early Western Australian settlements. Swan River Press.

The ship Rockingham – Passenger list
https://www.swanriverpioneers.com/the-ship-rockingham-14-may-1830

'Kick It Here!'

Lia Eliades

The boys play on the foreshore at Rockingham Beach, throwing jellyfish and sand bombs at each other. Suddenly, a ball bounces between them. The big brother picks it up, and the boys look up and see a man in the distance. He's waving his arms and smiling.

'Hey!' shouts the man. 'Kick it here!'

The boys do, and he swiftly kicks it back to them, smiling and nodding. The two brothers jostle for the ball.

The guy suddenly appears by their side, breathing heavily and laughing. He surveys the beach, swivelling his head as if looking out for someone. Eyeing the boys up and down, he stops, hands in pockets, and speaks. 'You guys here alone?'

The boys are silent. He looks up, quickly scans the horizon and smiles.

'Wanna play a game of soccer?' The man doesn't wait for an answer. 'Here, I'll mark some goals for us.' He drags the heel of his foot to make two goal post lines in the sand.

The boys look at each other and shrug.

'But there are only three of us, the teams won't be fair,' says the younger brother, squinting into the sun. He can see only a dark silhouette of the big man surrounded by light.

The man grins. 'Ah, that's okay; I'll take on the two of you.'

Both boys run along the shore towards the ball. They are quickly engaged in fancy footwork, kicking the ball towards the goal.

The man is grinning widely now and crouching down, waiting for the two boys as they make their way towards him. He grabs the younger boy around the waist and kind of tackles him, but doesn't let him go.

'Hey! No hands,' says the older brother. 'We're playing soccer, right? No tackling.'

The man looks up while still holding the younger brother in his arms; he drops his head into the crook of the boy's neck, and inhales deeply before he reluctantly lets him go.

The elder boy kicks the ball to his little brother, and they head in for a goal again, but the man is too good for them. He teases and tricks them, prancing the ball around them and through their legs, making them spin around in circles. He keeps the contact close, never lets them get too far from him. He laughs, nudges, and pushes the boys. From a distance, it looks like a young family having a bit of fun together.

If only that were true.

The three of them get into a tangle and fall onto the sand in a heap, laughing. The man brushes the hair of the young boy, smiling into his eyes. Their legs are entwined and he is squeezing the boys between his strong thighs. The brothers are shouting for mercy, the man is tickling them, laughing, calling them sissies.

'Can't get the ball, can't take the heat, it's two against one, you know.' The boys finally struggle free; the older boy perturbed, glares at the man. He grabs his brother and pulls him away from the man, looking back over his shoulder at him suspiciously.

'Come on, Harry, we gotta go home. Mum will be waiting.'

'No, no wait!' says the man, panic in his voice. He grabs Harry by the arm. 'I was just messing around. No tackling anymore. Come on, kick the ball.' He kicks it to the kids again; it hits them on their ankles as they start to walk away. Kai throws his arm around Harry's shoulder, pulling him in close, but Harry wriggles away from his older brother and turns around to return the ball with a big kick.

The man kicks the ball again, keeping Harry's attention on the ball; he doesn't allow the ball to rest, just keeps kicking it back and forth to Harry. The older brother is walking away now, shoulders slumped, head down, hands in pockets, and talking to himself. 'Stupid guy,' he says, 'you don't tackle in soccer.'

All of a sudden, he hears his brother scream.

He spins around in the direction of the scream, and sees Harry jumping up and down in a victory stance. 'GOAL! Score, score, I did it! Kai, I beat him! I got a goal.'

'Come on, Harry, we have to go.' Kai eyes the sun as it disappears behind a cloud on the horizon.

The man runs at a fast trot right up to Kai. 'Hey, Kai, Kai, listen, I'm gonna be here tomorrow afternoon if you want to have another game. You guys beat me today, so you need to promise to come back tomorrow, to give me a chance to even the score. Will you guys do that for me? It was fun, right? I mean, exercise is good for you. I can teach you some of the special tricks I know. I'll buy you guys an ice cream after, or get you a McDonald's if you want.' All of this he is saying as he follows closely on their heels as they make their way through the dunes.

'Hey, have you guys ever gone up there?' He points to the dunes. 'In the grasses here? I used to love to go there and pretend I was playing war, commando crawling around in the dunes with my friends. It was good fun. I used to love this place,' he sighs.

Harry says, 'That sounds cool. I would like to do that one day. I always wanted to, but Mum always says there are snakes in there, and all the signs say it is dangerous too.'

'We gotta go!' says Kai, grabbing the shoulder of Harry's T-shirt, pulling him towards home. A small bunny appears, quivering on the edge of the bush path. The man stops just before they get to the road, not wanting to be seen. He leans over and picks up the bunny in one hand.

'Hey, you guys, come here,' he says softly to their backs. 'Look, look what I've found.' His hand is extended out towards them. Harry runs back, Kai groans and follows, not wanting to let Harry out of his sight. Harry is looking into the man's palms at something.

'Isn't it cute?' The man speaks softly. 'Poor thing, no one to look after it, I wonder where its mother is? Poor defenceless little ones shouldn't be left alone like that.'

Harry is stroking the soft fur between the bunny's ears, when the man suddenly flings the little bunny into the air over the bush. 'Damn, ow,' he says nervously. 'He bit me, little bugger.' He tries to laugh it off, but he can see that Harry is distressed now. 'Don't worry, I am sure he's fine,' says the man. 'Do you want to go in there with me and look for him to check?'

'No!' says Kai. 'We have to go, it's dark.'

'Hey!' commands the man. 'You need to give me a handshake before you leave; that is good sportsmanship, to shake hands after a game.' The man is kneeling down in the sand now and shaking Harry's hand. 'Now listen, son, when you shake a man's hand, you look him in the eye and make sure you have a firm grip, no limp fish handshakes. A nice firm handshake.' The man is smiling broadly now as he holds Harry's hand in his, his eyes are sparkling, and his teeth shine from between beard. 'Nice to meet you, Harry. Thanks for the game. What about you?' says the man to Kai.

Kai walks towards the man with his head down and sticks his hand out.

'Did you hear what I told your brother? A man has to look a man in the eyes when he is shaking hands. Let's try that properly now.'

Kai is getting annoyed at this, but looks up into the man's eyes, and sees them all watery, filling with tears now. The man wipes at his face. 'I got some sand in my eyes,' he says. He blinks rapidly and clears his throat.

Kai looks at him quizzically. Something about the man is making him confused, making him scared. His brain is hurting, he's remembering something, the man's eyes, he just can't understand it. He winces.

'Nice to meet you, Kai; you're a fine young man.' He jerks Kai's hand and pulls him to his chest and puts his arm around his shoulder, patting his back. 'Good young man, you look out for your brother and be a good lad for your mum. She loves you, you know.'

'How do you know?' says Kai.

The man releases him and smiles, hands on hips now. 'Well, all mums do, it's their job. What about your dad?' says the man.

'What about him?' says Harry.

'Is he a good man?'

'I don't know,' says Harry.

'What does your mum say about him?'

'I never met him. He died.'

The man's face is stoic now; his smile disappears under his beard. He rubs the back of his neck firmly and his muscles burst up around his neck and shoulders.

Kai says, 'Yeah, he died, and now we have to go.'

The man, despondent on his knees as the boys walk away, muffles a cry into his shirt sleeve.

He stands up in time to shout to the boys once more. 'Here,' he says, 'you guys keep the ball – a gift from me.' He throws it to them in an overhand pass. 'Something to remember me by.'

'Won't you be back tomorrow?' says Harry. 'We can have another game tomorrow, like you said.'

'I don't know,' he says, 'I might have to go to work, but you guys keep practising; you were pretty good out there.'

Harry shrugs, takes the ball under his arm and waves thanks to the man. Kai wraps an arm around his shoulder, and they bump against each other as they walk into the distance across the darkened street, then through the glow of the streetlamp and disappear from sight for the last time, into the void of non-existence again.

***

The man gets back into his car and calls Marina.

'How did it go?' she asks.

The man bursts into tears. 'She told them I was dead; she fucking told them I was dead. The bunny ... I probably killed it.'

'What?' says Marina, confused now.

'My boys ... you should have seen them, Marina. So beautiful. Kai, so big now; smart kid, so beautiful. And Harry, all personality, good with a soccer ball too, reminds me of me when I was his age.'

'Tom, what bunny? What are you talking about? Did you tell them? Did you tell them that you're their father?'

'How could I? They think I'm dead; it's too confusing for them. I ... I didn't know what to do. I let them walk away ... I just had to let them walk away. Marina, my heart is breaking; I can't breathe, I just can't.'

She hears only a small choking sound, a whimper. 'Tom? Tom, are you all right?'

'I don't know. I don't feel so good; I'm so tired.' He feels nauseous. Tom sees white flashes before his eyes; he now has a searing headache and his neck aches.

'Tom, come back to the hotel. Tom, do you hear me?'

He is gasping now, looking for breath, repeating his son's names. 'They think I'm dead.'

Tom slumps over the steering wheel.

Marina repeats his name over and over, 'Tom! Talk to me, Tom. Where are you? I'm coming. Tom! Tom!'

The phone falls to the floor.

Licence To Remember

Jean Frost

The licensing centre across the road from the Rockingham Police Station was unexpectedly busy the day Edward Graham pulled his old Ford Anglia up to the kerb. 'There you go,' he said affectionately, patting the steering wheel. 'And they said you didn't have it in you.'

'Oh, come on, Dad,' his middle-aged son said from the passenger seat. 'It was a joke, and I said I was sorry.'

Ed turned to face his son. 'I didn't think it was amusing being accused of losing my marbles, especially when you consider what happened to your aunt Mary. And you know how I feel about that.'

'Of course, I don't think you're losing your marbles. Anyone could forget to renew their driver's licence; heck, even me. What do you want me to say?'

'Nothing,' Ed bit back. 'You don't need to say another word. Go. Do your shopping, and I'll call you when I'm finished.'

He watched his son disappear down the road before turning his attention to the multi-storey building on the other side of the street. He couldn't get over how sterile it looked, with its layers of glass and steel, not at all like the old police station on Smythe Street, where he first got his licence all those years ago. 'Now, all I need is to pass this ruddy test, and I'll prove my marbles are in their right place,' he muttered after carefully getting out of the car. His knees weren't at all what they used to be back in his younger days, a fact he was struggling to accept.

'Ticket number 351 to the eye test area.'

Ed cringed at the metallic-sounding voice coming from an overhead speaker and looked at the number on the ticket he had retrieved from the machine when he entered. It was his number, and he slowly rose to make his way as instructed.

'Ok, Mr Graham, please read the third line from the bottom.'

Ed shuffled forward to place the tips of his brown loafers on the edge of the green line and cleared his throat. 'Third line, you said?'

'Yes, please, from the bottom, if you will.'

Ed pulled his shoulders back and sucked in a deep breath. He hoped this move would show his confidence, as he needed to get it right. The thought of continually relying on his son to drive him everywhere gave him the chills, as his constant whinging was a nightmare. Adjusting his glasses so they sat near the bridge of his nose rather than resting on the bulbous tip, he quickly glanced at the young woman standing beside the eye test chart and estimated her age to be close to that of his granddaughters. Not that it mattered to him one way or the other, but there was a slim possibility that she had a grandfather about the same age and might cut him some slack if he got one or two of the letters wrong.

Giving the eye chart his full attention, Ed licked his lips to make sure they weren't stuck together and spoke in the most confident tone he could muster. 'T… D… R… S… A… And I think it is Q?' giving a little chuckle in the hope he sounded nonchalant.

***

He watched as the young woman jotted something down on the score sheet and cringed inwardly. Why couldn't he have just said the letter 'Q' instead of 'I think', as it made him sound dithery and unsure of what he saw?

'Ok, I think we've got everything. Please, take this.' The young woman handed him the page she had scribbled on. 'The Driver Assessor will call you when it is your turn.'

He eyed the confusion of blue lines sitting beside one box, but couldn't make out what it said. The sudden urge to retrieve his reading glasses flitted through his mind, but he immediately dismissed the idea, as he didn't want to attract any further attention. In the end, he collected his walking stick from where he had left it and went to find a seat.

Oh dear, he thought after rounding the central pillar that separated the eye-testing cubicles from the waiting area. The place was packed. Every single chair was occupied by someone, either on their mobile phones or watching one of the TV screens hanging from the ceiling. Dots of perspiration appeared on his forehead as he slowly backed up to lean against the wall.

'Excuse me, mate.'

The deep voice came from Ed's left. When he looked around to see who the man was talking to, he saw a tall, heavy-set man with a crew cut looking in his direction.

'Here,' the man said, pointing to an empty chair behind him, 'You can take my chair. It looks like you need it more than I do.'

Ed smiled, full of gratitude, as he knew his knees wouldn't have held him up for much longer, and gingerly hobbled over to plonk himself down. 'Thank you,' he wheezed while wiping his forehead with a handkerchief. 'The old knees aren't what they used to be.'

The crewcut man nodded knowingly and pointed to a knee brace he was sporting himself. 'Football,' was all he said.

Ed swallowed the bubbles of guilt that threatened to rise. He wished he could stay there, resting his knees and preparing for the gruelling driving test to come. But he now felt as guilty as hell. He needed to do the right thing. He positioned his walking stick, ready to take his weight, when the PA system burst into life.

'That's me,' the crewcut man called out after hearing his name and hurried over to talk to a woman behind the counter.

With a sigh, Ed relaxed back in the chair, relieved he didn't have to give it up after all, and closed his eyes. The theme from *Days of Our Lives* floated through a speaker and immediately took him back to the small family home where his wife refused to miss an episode of her midday soap. He remembered how devastated she was when they finally took the serial off the air—it was hell for a few months that year, that was for sure.

'Edward Graham to window seven, please,' announced a warm female voice over the PA system.

Ed struggled to his feet and shuffled off as instructed.

It took a few moments to get there, but when Ed finally arrived, a tall, middle-aged man dressed in a grey dust coat stood behind the counter. 'Hi, I'm Steve, your driving assessor. Do you have your eye test?'

Ed had forgotten all about the paper and swore under his breath. Now, he would never know what the woman had scribbled, but as the instructor ran his eyes down the list of boxes, he smiled. 'Everything looks in order, so let's find your car and get started.'

***

'I can't wait to tell my dad I sat in a 1965 Ford Anglia today,' Steve said, after running his hand over the dashboard of Ed's car for the umpteenth time. 'It will blow his mind. It's his all-time favourite.' He then coughed a laugh and turned to Ed. 'There's this old, dog-eared photo that he whips out every time we talk about cars. He tells me the same story over and over. It drives me crazy, and he knows it.'

Ed lovingly caressed the top of the steering wheel as he felt his insides settle. His old car had come to his rescue once more. 'Yes,

I know how your dad feels. Old Gertie here has got me through some tight situations. She just keeps going where others might have given up the ghost.'

Steve gave the dash one last pat as he slid the buckle of the seatbelt into place. 'Ok, enough of all this sentimental stuff. I'm here to help you get your licence back. So, when you're ready, I want you to turn right at these lights.' He pointed to the set of traffic lights directly in front of them. '… and then turn right at the next set onto Read Street. Have you got that?'

Ed snickered. 'Right, then right. Right, it is.' He shook his head slightly, silently chastising himself. He really needed to think before opening his mouth, as his son would always remind him about the fine line between humour and sarcasm. To calm his nerves, he put on a show of checking his mirrors, just like in the YouTube clips he had watched to brush up on his road rules, before flicking on the indicator and, without hesitation, pulling away from the kerb. The manoeuvre couldn't have gone more smoothly, and before long, they were turning onto Read Street.

'Perfect,' Steve said as he ticked a box on his clipboard. 'Now, I want you to turn left at the second set of lights down the road.'

Ed eased his grip on Gertie's steering wheel. The last thing he wanted was to squeeze the life out of the old girl, and he made a mental note to give her an extra coat of wax the next time he took her through the car wash.

'How long have you lived in the area?' Steve asked.

'Well, let's see.' Without taking his eyes off the road, Ed nodded towards the group of buildings surrounded by a wire fence on his left. 'Before that was there.'

Steve looked in the direction Ed had pointed. 'Rockingham High School, you mean? Wow, quite a few years ago, then. My dad was among the first students at what was then called "First Year High". They call it "Year 8" now.'

'I had to do my first two years at Kwinana High School, and then only did half a year at Rockingham. I left to get a job. Learnt more getting my hands dirty than what any teacher could have taught me.' He shrugged to emphasise that not everyone was an academic and then asked, 'You said turn left at the lights coming up, didn't you?'

'Yes,' Steve said, 'and then proceed to the foreshore.'

Ed waited until they had passed all the other turn-ins before flicking on his indicator. It was one thing his son had constantly harped on, saying he put his indicator on too early and that one day it would cause an accident. He made the turn without stopping. For once, the lights were in his favour. Out of the corner of his eye, he saw Steve tick another box.

'I bet you have seen a lot of changes down here as well?'

As much as Ed loved to strut down memory lane, enjoying reminiscing about growing up in a small tourist town like Rockingham, he knew he had to keep his mind on the game and not get sidetracked by Steve's chatty nature. A sudden thought crossed his mind. *Is the chitchat a ploy to throw me off my game? Is Steve distracting me to see if I will slip up?* Well, he was wasting his time because it wouldn't happen. So, he didn't answer the question right away. He wanted to take his time and focus on what he was doing. After stopping at the lights, he took a controlled breath and said, 'Everyone who grew up here back in the day had a fantastic time. On the corner here,' he gestured to his right, 'there used to be a caravan park called Sun Ray. It was a small place with only about twenty bays, and it was always full. And down there...' He pointed to the foreshore but didn't get the chance to finish his sentence as the lights turned green.

'Ok,' Steve said after they had made it through the lights, and slapped his folder shut with a snap. The sudden action sparked a sharp bubble of acidic dread to rise in Ed's chest. Without realising it, his shoulders curled inward, acting as a shield. *There you go, I knew it. Just a ploy to throw me off my game.* But what had he done wrong? He waited a respectful two seconds after the light had turned green before driving off. He hadn't rushed. No jerking, nothing. So, what?

'Now comes the big one,' Steve continued. 'I'd like to see how you handle parallel parking. So, I want you to drive along the foreshore and take the next right. When you find a suitable space near the hotel, I want you to park the car.'

Ed exhaled with relief. Parallel parking was his least favourite thing about driving, usually avoiding it at all costs, but he knew it would come up at least once in the test. So, he had practised.

***

The parking spot opposite the old Rockingham Hotel looked perfect. Ed estimated that the space between the Nissan Patrol, with its enormous black bull bar and a tall whip aerial rising like a flagpole to meet the sky, and a small black-and-white checkered Mini, could easily accommodate a limousine. Parking old Gertie would be a breeze. He pulled the Ford Anglia alongside the Mini and checked his mirror for oncoming traffic. In the reflection, the sparkling waters of Mangles Bay, and in the background, the familiar haze of Garden Island caught his eye. Momentarily distracted, he thought back to a time in his youth when he usually met up with friends in the hotel's beer gardens for the Sunday Session. There would always be a live local band belting out their version of a cover from any group that had made it to that week's top ten on the charts. Even back then, he loved looking at the island.

'Umm, Ed?' Steve's voice cut through Ed's reverie, and he blinked a few times to clear his thoughts. 'Are you still with us?'

'Sorry,' Ed coughed. 'It's just with all this talk about the past and what Rockingham was like back in the day, I got a little sidetracked.'

'Understandable, but we can't sit in the middle of the road all day,' Steve gestured towards the kerb, without opening his mouth again. Ed reversed the car and finished parking.

Steve opened his door and checked how close they were to the kerb. 'I think I've seen all I need. You can take us back to the licensing centre via the roundabout on Louise Street now, thanks, Ed.'

Louise Street? Where the hell is that? Ed looked down at the steering wheel and frowned. He had never paid much attention to the names of the streets around the area. If he were going to the shops, for example, he would have said, 'Meet me at Rocko shops,' or 'Hey, I'm going to Bunnings.' Everyone knew where those places were, so there was no need for street names. Quickly bringing up a mental map of the area, he decided it must be the one on the way to Bunnings. So, with his fingers crossed, he pulled Gertie away from the kerb, and they were on their way.

***

'Well, how do you reckon you went today?' Steve asked after Ed pulled up at the kerb, applied the handbrake, and killed the engine.

Ed sat there for a few moments, jingling the keys in his hand. He thought he had done well, but forgetting to signal when leaving the roundabout was a big mistake. That, and sitting in the middle of the road like a zombie. What had he been thinking, or better still, not thinking? Either could cost him dearly, and he silently sent up a prayer to the car gods that Steve would not penalise him for that. 'I think I did all right. I know I need to brush up on the whole roundabout thing, and I intend to.'

'Yeah, good idea. But I've got something to ask you.'

Ed shifted slightly in his seat, curious about what might come next. 'I'm having a barbecue this weekend for my dad's birthday. We think it will be his last since he's got stage four cancer and isn't doing too well. I want to do something extra special for him. I know this is a lot to ask, but it would mean the world to him if you came and brought this old girl along.'

Without hesitation, Ed agreed.

'Ok then,' Steve said as he extended his hand. 'Let's get the paperwork done, and you on your way.'

Mangles, Mangles Bay

Rosanne Dingli

We came into the township at dead of night, when no one was astir. It wasn't as small as I'd thought. Clopping down the main street, from where I swore I could see the black glimmer of water in the distance, I felt we would wake every living soul; hoof beats and the rumble of cartwheels can be heard miles away at night, and the houses on that street had doors not four feet from the gutter. But not a face showed itself, and no lamplight was visible behind windows we passed.

'Where are we?' whispered one of the children.

'What's this place called?' Johnny asked in a low voice.

'Didn't you see the sign as we came in? This is Rockingham.'

He shook his capped head, and put the cold pipe between his teeth. About a month before, when money ran short, he reduced his smoking to one pipe a day, after supper. 'Couldn't be. It should be further south a bit.'

'But I read it.'

'Me too,' piped a little voice from under the canvas cloth on the back of the cart.

Johnny laughed. 'He can *read* now, that little whippersnapper.' He took the first right turn he could and we were moving out, past a clutch of sheds, they looked like, and then the grassed rise of dunes. Our lantern swung and caused everything to move as if of its own accord. 'Looks like another night on the beach, Mother.'

I hated it when he did that, calling me Mother when his own was still alive. Well, alive somewhere. We hadn't heard she wasn't. But we left our old north town, the old stone house, three doors up from her, a good few months before, when Johnny was pursued by the Wrexham boys for money he didn't owe.

'I paid it back, Nora. Honest, I did. But there weren't no witnesses. And they're after me for it. Still. *Again.*'

I almost, at the time, said, *Serve you right, Johnny, for borrowing in the first place*. But no wife should be that cruel. He did it to feed us. And we ate for a week or two until he found road work out where they said a highway was coming in.

But the Wrexhams kept coming back. When his mother opened the door they were sweet as pie. 'We don't want nothin' from ye, old lady. Just Johnny. Where's that Johnny?'

It wasn't going to go away. So we piled all we owned and the three children onto the cart, thanked Phil Marson for the old nag he gave us for my wedding ring, and we started down towards the river, three days away. Three days, they said. It took us ages longer. We had to go east, ever eastward to find a bridge over, but we did eventually, next to a flourmill and a tannery. Or it could have been a slaughterhouse, but the smell was there.

'The further south we go, the better the weather. Another two days should do it. It was too hot for ye there, weren't it?' He champed on the pipe end, making it sound like we left because I couldn't stand the heat. Well, no matter why, we did leave, and his mother stayed on, and that was no loss to me.

Another two days, he said. It took us ages more.

'Perhaps we'll get somewhere we can farm a bit. Grow something?' The lightness I felt could have been hope.

'We'd have to rent a place for that. No money, Nora. I'll have to find work.'

We lived on the beach just below Rockingham.

'Just for a few days.' Johnny was ever the optimist.

We were there for ages. For more than a few *weeks*, behind some rocks, in a patch of bush. We draped the canvas over the cart and slept under it, the five of us.

The children got as brown as berries, and caught plenty of whiting with some old line found in the sand and hooks they wheedled from goodhearted fishermen.

Just when I was starting to ask myself what we had done, an old angler pointed out an abandoned beach shack up behind the dunes.

'Surely not,' I said under my breath.

'Oh, *surely*,' he said. 'That was Peter Yew and his new wife's, that hut. She wouldna stay under corrugated tin. Not that lady. So he took her north, he did. A good year ago now. Up north.' I had to laugh at that.

So we fixed it up, me putting aside the thought of being squatters, the children not knowing what the word meant. We made it right, Johnny's good that way, and I have a pair of hands that never waved a spade or a hammer or a broom away. The children were fine, especially when they dragged home wood for a fire, or some old empty can we could rinse out, or three hessian sacks someone let them have at the store. Had a few holes, but no matter. I picked them out flat in the evenings, until the light went. They made a good curtain, before we got another sheet of canvas.

And then Johnny came back from town saying they were taking on men to load timber onto ships.

'Timber?'

'Ships!'

'Yeah, we saw them out there, didn't we, boys? Past that rocky point, see? And there *is* a railway. That man at the bridge was right. Train comes along from a place called Jarrahdale, loaded with logs and planks and all manner of lumber.' He looked at the fish I was gutting, and the greens I had pulled from a patch I found along the beach path. 'Can you eat them greens?'

We'd eaten them before, and they did us no harm, but he always asked.

'If the work's regular like, Nora, we'll get a place. How does that sound?'

'Sounds good,' I had to admit.

'It's not bad loading at Mangles.'

'*Mangles?*' He had a name for everything.

'I didn't make that one up. Ask anyone you like. No! I promise ... Mangles. Mangles Bay.'

I did ask. There was a woman who walked by with a basket of washing every now and then who knew everything. 'That'll be the name of that fancy family. You know. The daughter ... the Mangles daughter*. Some years back. Married Governor Stirling.' She made a face, meaning we should be impressed. 'You know, what—twelve, thirteen, twenty year ago now? That fancy Mangles family, yeah.'

So Johnny was right, and I learned something.

The woman looked at my makeshift clothesline, strung from the shack to a branch. 'Looks like you're doing all right, yerself.'

And she gave a side smile. 'But just give us a shout if you're not.'

Oh, we were fine. I felt things were going fine.

And then the inspector came down, to talk to me. 'One, two ... and is that one a girl? Is she yours?'

I had to crop her hair short, but sure, Meg was a girl all right, and mine, mine. 'Three,' I said to him, knowing what his next words would be.

'School, missus. From after Easter. School, for the three of 'em. How old's the girlie?'

'Mark's nearly ten, Jon-Jon's eight, and Meggie's seven soon.'

'School!' And he marched off, unsteady on the sand. 'You know where it is.' When he turned, I knew what he would say then, too. 'And you can't ...' he called, but stopped. 'Look—it's none of my business where you stay.'

If Johnny hadn't said the work looked regular, I'd have worried, but I knew he'd keep his word and get us a place.

We took the cart with all the children on as far as the school in Rockingham, and got them written up. Meggie didn't like the master's 'sour face', she called it, but you should have seen her eyes when she saw the slates and chalk and books and pictures on the walls and the stove in the corner. We had to pull her back down those front steps. 'Ye'll all come back Monday, lovie!'

And Johnny took what he called the long way back, slowing down and pointing at a small place with a crooked gate in a wire fence. 'Look, Mark, look, Jon-Jon. Hey, Meggie ... see the house? How's that for starters, Mother?'

And that's how we got settled. Our place was on the bend right up from Mangles Bay, backing up to the lake where all the birds were, so Johnny could walk to work and back swinging a lunch pail and an old beer bottle full of tea, and run back home if it was raining too hard to work.

It took a while, and we had to get some windowpanes replaced, but we were given a lot of things. Neighbours provided an old kitchen sieve, a washing board, an enamel basin a bit bigger than mine, two brooms someone left behind, a proper teapot, and a hand-sewn mattress we struggled with from round the corner to the back room where the boys slept. It was almost like everyone enjoyed getting us settled, because there wasn't a week I didn't find something left for us by the gate. And there wasn't a week I didn't make a batch of rock cakes and send them round with the children.

When Johnny came home with a brand-new spade and hoe from the store, I couldn't believe my luck. Even luckier when he put a little brass ring on my finger. 'Happy now, Nora?'

I dug all the yard up on my own, when the children were at school, because they went there and back each day on the wagon with the Bells.

I put in what I could, mostly beans at first, but they came up good.

And then I straightened the gate.

Johnny said our landlord was an old Chinaman, but I never saw him, and never believed him. He made some things into jokes, but I made sure he was down the road with the money every month. I was taking no risks.

In time, the children were the cleanest, sweetest, cleverest little things in the school, all shod proper and everything. They knew their turns to sit on the shaky wooden crate out the back veranda to get their heads checked. I wasn't having no nits in my beds.

Johnny settled. His back broadened because of the hauling, his face tanned and his hair went a bit grey under the cloth cap, but he was right and straight, and never borrowed another penny.

He'd come home, sometimes after dark, throw the children up one by one in the air until they were too big for it, and shout them a question, before he lit his pipe. 'And where do we all live then?'

And they would shout back, *'Mangles! Mangles Bay!'*

***

*Lady Ellen Stirling
https://www.portrait.gov.au/portraits/2008.53/ellen-stirling

Me and Mike

(Life before credit cards and after pay)

Bernadette Piper

Hot air swirled around me; the grass under the tall eucalyptus trees was dotted with families on rugs. Seagulls fought over scraps, their squawking drowned out by screeching white cockatoos as they flew from tree to tree. Kids yelled and ran across the sand to cool their feet in the blue ocean—the usual sounds of summer in Rockingham.

I stood leaning on the rusty railing, looking across the water at Garden Island, now a Navy Base, no longer accessible to civilians. Taking deep breaths, I squared my shoulders and walked away, following the shoreline and then across the grass to do something I'd never done before.

***

The bracelet was the most difficult. I guess the first time at anything is the most difficult. The phone call of enquiry, the casual approach to the counter, the nervous laughter.

His shop was out of the way, down Kent Street, not far from the old Rockingham Hotel. Red brick walls and scratchy glass windows covered in mesh wire. Musty dust in the air, all the floor space occupied with old bits of furniture, musical instruments, records and players, cameras, bits and pieces—an Aladdin's Cave.

The glass-topped counter was full of dreams, and broken hearts, jewellery and watches, which someone had loved, sold off or never reclaimed.

'How much can I borrow against this?' I asked, glancing around, hoping no one I knew would come into the shop.

He didn't take long to look at the bracelet. I knew it was worth a little bit; Jamie had given it to me one year after we met, before mortgages and interest rates.

'$40.00. I can loan you $40.00 or buy it from you for $80.00.'

I ran my hand around the bracelet, swallowing my tears. 'No, no, I can't sell it.'

'A loan then … $40.00.'

'Yes.'

He held the bracelet in his chubby hand. His brown eyes and crooked smile tried to reassure me. 'It will be safe here, probably safer than at home.'

I had to show him identification on this occasion—a driver's license without a photograph, a licence that could have belonged to anyone. I signed the paper, and he gave me the pink slip and $40.00.

I rushed out the door, hoping no one I knew saw me. *Surely, no one is in the same predicament as we are. Not anyone we know, anyway.*

I felt like a millionaire. I had paper money in my pocket for the first time in a week. When Joshua asked, 'Mummy, can I have an ice cream?' I could say yes instead of growling, 'I have no money.'

***

The next time I visited Mike, I was bolder, walking in, not looking around, only a little nervous laughter and quiet enquiry.

'How much can I borrow against this?'

Granddad's ring, very old and heavy, solid 18ct gold.

'Yes, I can loan you $80.00 against the ring.'

I picked up my bracelet and had the balance to see us through to payday. We still call it *payday* at our house. Pension day doesn't seem right when you are a young couple.

The watch didn't raise enough to collect the ring.

I was bold with the necklace.

It was only silver with green glass stones. It was gorgeous and I loved it, but I knew it wasn't worth much. I went straight to the counter, not looking around; no nervous laughter. 'How much can I have against this?'

Mike took his time with the necklace. He pulled an eyeglass from a drawer and studied it.

'Have you had it long?'

I hoped to get enough money to buy food for the children. Sweat ran along my palms. 'Not long, just a few years. Isn't it worth anything?'

'It's very old, and it's not silver, it's platinum.'

Platinum. I knew that was expensive.

'The stones are real, too.'

'Real?'

'They are emeralds.'

'Emeralds?'

'I can loan you up to $500.00 on this.'

Dust filled my lungs. *$500.00.* I knew Mike only ever loaned 10% of the value of any item he advanced against. We were on a first-name basis, having become acquainted across his shop counter over the months, and I had become an expert over time.

'Can I have $200.00?' I mumbled.

Two hundred dollars. Enough to reclaim the watch and the ring and keep us afloat. We jest with each other, me and Mike. 'One day, when I'm rich and famous, I will write about you in my memoirs.'

He laughed. 'Yes, you'll tell everyone how I ripped you off.'

'No, how you kept me going.' And that was the truth.

Maybe I should have taken the $500.00, but there had to be hope, and $200.00 would be easier to repay. I might be able to afford the interest: 20% of the loan amount, paid monthly. But I didn't expect to see Mike again.

I had the bracelet, the ring and the watch. There was nothing of more value than the necklace.

Grandma had left it to her beloved grandson, the boy who would carry her husband's name on. That had been important to her. We'd thought it a sentimental gesture, but Jamie had cherished it, and I would wear it on special occasions.

I hoped Grandma would forgive me. She was a practical woman, having lived through the Depression and two wars, and I believed she would understand, if not forgive.

'Heather,' Mike called as I stood with my hand on the door, holding it against the ever-blowing wind. 'Don't forget I keep the goods for three months before I put them out to sell.'

'No, I won't forget.'

I did see Mike once again. Two weeks later, Jamie got a job on the industrial strip in Kwinana, with two weeks' pay in advance and Mike and I met again. I gave him the pink slip, signed the white copy, and retrieved the necklace.

'It looks good, back where it belongs.' He helped me fasten the clasp around my neck. 'It matches your eyes, too.'

***

When Sarah was born four weeks later in Rockingham General Hospital, I received a small posy of wildflowers with a note that simply said, 'Mike.'

Murder They Cried

Sue Sacchero

Resplendent in wig and gown, ne'er before worn in Perth, Mr Nash concluded the case for the defence.

In the new courthouse, packed to capacity for the final day of my trial for the murder of my infant son, the hoi polloi jostled for places with the eager gentlemen of the press. Public interest had not waned over the three months since I'd been charged. Speculation about my likely fate was the relentless talk of the town.

With much pomp, the highly esteemed Advocate General, Mr George Fletcher Moore, rose unhurriedly to address the Court.

The restless crowd fell silent as a tepid trickle of perspiration ran down my back. My nerve slipped away. I flinched and felt goosebumps run down my arms as though someone had walked over the grave I feared I'd soon occupy. My heart froze, then pounded. I wanted to remain aloof, disconnected, and suppress the unsettling emotions that strove to control me.

Mr Moore cleared his throat with learnt deliberation.

'If the talents and ingenuity of the defence could do away with the truth, I must confess, the prisoner has a very good chance of acquittal,' he proclaimed with undisguised cynicism. 'To a very great extent untruths have been asserted by the defence on her behalf.' He fixed the Chairman of the Jury with a practised theatrical glare.

Pausing for greater effect, eyes still bulging, he stepped forward and, in a firm voice, proceeded with the confidence of his station.

'Unless you are prepared to disbelieve the evidence of Mrs Charlotte Whitfield the Jury can come to no other conclusion than that the prisoner is guilty of murder!'

Mr Nash had warned me to expect this; nonetheless, I stiffened trying to suppress an inexplicable urge for uncontrolled laughter.

The Advocate General continued to argue forcibly; I hardly took in anything of his very able speech. Although I do recall he briefly alluded to the fact that perhaps I was not completely of sound mind at the time my baby was delivered. I had no doubt my chances of escaping the gallows were slim indeed. At barely seventeen, I fully expected to have the dubious honour of being the first white person to be executed in the Swan River Colony.

'Furthermore,' the Advocate General continued, 'the medical witness, Dr Joseph Harris, did not show, in the case of Miss Green, delirium had actually existed. He merely stated that it usually existed in cases such as hers.' He hesitated. 'The entire defence case has rested on this proposition. I beg the Jury not to take it for more than it is worth.'

Another pregnant pause followed.

'There was method in her madness. The whole of Miss Green's conduct has been of artful and positive design. After a display of cunning and perseverance she used various endeavours to conceal the facts.' He waited, ensuring he had the full attention of every juror.

'It is too much to hope to make the Jury believe Miss Green was not of sound mind at the time. We have heard the girl used all her exertions to effect a concealment and has shown considerable fortitude in order to obtain such a result. There can be no doubt of clear malicious intent!'

Then, in the strongest terms, the honourable gentlemen urged the Jury to do their duty.

With a pounding heart, my shaking legs barely supported me. Looking straight ahead, I silently repeated my prayers. My only consolation was my nightmare of the past year would soon be over.

As my mind replayed everything that had occurred since I'd been assigned to the Whitfields, the Chairman, the handsome, highly esteemed Mr William Mackie, commenced his summing up.

'After the full and temperate manner in which the particulars have been stated on the part of the Crown, and after the ability and ingenuity displayed by the learned gentleman Mr Nash, for the defence, there remains little for the Court to say.'

As he spoke, I caught Mrs Knott's eye. She'd been sitting with Reverend Wittenoom during every moment of the trial. She returned a discreet, reassuring grin. If I were to be saved from the gallows, it would be because of the efforts of these pious citizens. They would be my salvation. They had done everything in their power to assist me. Mrs Knott, the superintendent of the orphans sent out on the *Eleanor*, had stood by me with much-appreciated solace and support.

Dear Reverend Wittenoom was one of the few commissioners who'd been appointed by the governor to protect the interest of orphans sent to the Colony that took their role seriously; sparing no effort he'd organised the best legal assistance possible for me.

Mr Mackie resumed. 'I should merely draw your attention to particular points which are necessary in order that you reach the right verdict.'

Anxious to know what these might be, I paid close attention.

'The jury must be satisfied,' he maintained, 'firstly, the child was born alive; secondly, the fatal injuries were inflicted by the prisoner; and thirdly, she inflicted them being in a sound state of mind.'

There was no option other than to put my faith in the skills of Mr Nash. I understood these were the three issues that must be proved if I were to be condemned to death.

'If you believe the evidence of Mrs Whitfield, the first point is settled.' My heart sank as Mr Mackie carried on. 'Of the second point, there can be no reasonable doubt. In fact, the point was admitted by the prisoner's counsel, and thus the third point is the thing you must consider. You have heard the evidence given on the subject, and it remains for you to give your verdict on it. If you entertain any doubts whatsoever as to the state of mind of the girl, it is your duty to give the prisoner the benefit of such doubts. I beg you to give your verdict according to the evidence. If you think it insufficient to support the plea of temporary insanity, you must act accordingly. Do not be led away by your feelings.'

The jury retired to consider its verdict.

Author's note. Jane Green married James Bell in 1847, and together they became Rockingham pioneers.

Old Goldie

Dianne Johnson

The Golden Labrador stood majestically at the bow of the boat, his front paws on the edge and his face to the wind. If dogs smile, then Goldie did. He was enjoying the excursion as much as Paul and Beth.

'Like to have a swim, Beth? There's a little beach not far from here, it's just around the point.'

'Sounds great!' Beth reapplied another layer of sunblock to her glowing English complexion. How she loved Western Australia, especially Rockingham. She looked at Paul. His day-old whiskers seemed to further enhance his rugged look. He was so handsome. She knew that her holiday was fast coming to an end, and all too soon she would have to say goodbye to the new man in her life. Her mind drifted. How she wished she could capture this moment forever.

Snapping from her daydream, Beth realised the weather had changed. A wind seemed to come from nowhere. Soon, the little boat was riding the swell. Although it was a bit rough, Beth enjoyed the ride. She laughed as each wave splashed sea spray onto her face.

As they rounded the point, the small sandy beach came into view. Goldie curled himself up and lay quietly on the coiled anchor rope. The wind grew stronger, and the waves increased as the tiny boat inched closer to shore.

Paul felt nervous. Never had he experienced such a sudden change in weather conditions, and he became quiet as he piloted the craft towards shore.

Suddenly, the motor spluttered and stopped. 'Must be seaweed caught in the blades.' He leaned over to release it. But it was no use. The motor was dead. He tried to restart it, but without success.

Beth held on tightly. She looked down at her feet, now bathed in seawater, and shivered. Waves tossed the small boat, pushing it further out.

'We're close enough,' Paul yelled. 'Let's swim for the shore.'

'But I can't swim!' Beth replied fearfully.

Sizing up the situation, Paul jumped overboard and, clutching the guide rope, headed for land, dragging the small boat behind.

Progress was slow in the choppy water. Goldie whimpered uncharacteristically as if he could sense danger.

With painstaking effort, Paul relentlessly swam on, inching his precious load nearer and nearer towards the shore.

Beth felt useless and helpless in the precarious situation. She shivered, chilled from the cold wind and fear. How quickly the scene had changed. One minute they were laughing with joy, the next they were shaking in terror.

The sandy bottom became visible, but the breakers continued to buffet the tiny boat. They were so close to shore. So close, and yet it seemed so far. Paul was tiring as he negotiated the opposing waves. Suddenly, a large wave turned the boat sideways, but before Paul recovered enough to face the boat into the waves, another freak wave hit, tossing the vessel high. Beth and Goldie were thrown aimlessly, like rag toys, into the sea. The boat came down with a mighty thud, pinning Paul momentarily to the sandy seabed. The receding wave dragged the capsized boat off his limp body.

The next thing Beth remembered was waking to the sound of distant sirens and being comforted by a stranger on the beach. 'Don't be afraid, dear; everything will be fine.' His words brought warmth and reassurance, and although she was still shaken, she somehow sensed that all would be well.

An ambulance arrived. One officer hurried to aid Paul and the other checked Beth.

'How is Paul?' she asked, turning to the stranger.

'He's unconscious, but alive. So don't you worry, dear; he's in good hands.'

'And the dog? What about Goldie? Have you seen him?' The stranger looked at the worried girl, and in tender tones, he described the heroic sacrifice old Goldie had made. He told how, although badly injured himself, the faithful dog had returned to the water, first dragging Beth, then Paul, from the sea and certain death. 'Once he knew you were both safe,' continued the stranger, 'the dog laid his broken, bleeding body on the sand, gave a final sigh, and died.'

'Oh no,' sobbed Beth, 'it can't be, not Goldie!' Sorrow stabbed like a knife in her heart. *I'm to blame,* she thought. *It's all my fault. If it wasn't for me, Paul wouldn't have even gone out today.*

The stranger held her close and, as if knowing her thoughts, he said, 'You're not responsible my dear. It was an accident, and no one is to blame.'

Beth sighed, and resting her head against his chest, once again found comfort in the voice of the stranger.

A second ambulance arrived. Quickly, the paramedic immobilised Beth's neck, bandaged her head, and carried her by stretcher to the waiting ambulance. A police officer questioned her briefly, but Beth suggested he speak to the man on the beach, since he had seen the whole thing. 'What man?' the policeman queried.

Turning her eyes, Beth realised that her friend had gone.

'Did you see where he went?' she asked the ambulance driver.

'Beats me,' he replied, scratching his head.

'He was right here a moment ago. It's like he just vanished!'

'It'll be okay,' the policeman assured them. 'He'll probably come forward when we issue the call for eyewitnesses.'

Beth propped herself up and glanced back towards the beach, hoping to get one last glimpse of the stranger, but he had gone. The doors of the ambulance closed, and she drifted into a dazed sleep.

***

Beth's injuries were minor compared to Paul's, and she was released from the hospital the next day. Her scheduled return to England was postponed, as she couldn't bear to leave Paul's side. His life hung in the balance. Paul's parents kept vigil, hoping, praying, and waiting. The medical team were doing all they could, but the outcome was uncertain.

Days stretched into weeks; Paul's condition swung like a pendulum, one day, a glimmer of hope, the next, another setback.

New Year's Eve came, but for Beth, there was no party. She sat by Paul's bedside; the only sound breaking the silence was the machine keeping him alive. He lay in a deep coma, pale and gaunt; a mere shadow of the robust young man she had met less than a month before.

Her thoughts wandered, and tears filled her eyes as she thought about Goldie and how brave he had been. Then she thought about the stranger on the beach. Who was he? And why didn't he answer the police call for him to come forward as an eyewitness? She thought about the mysterious message received at the Ambulance headquarters. It was the voice of the stranger, registered at 1:27 pm. Yet, both Paul's and her watches were smashed on impact, and both read 1:33 pm! Was the message received before the accident happened?

Deep in thought, she hardly noticed the slight flicker of Paul's eyelids. He caught her attention though, when, ever so faintly, he whispered her name. She leant over and kissed him tenderly. Tears streamed down her cheeks. 'Oh, Paul, you're awake.' She could say no more, the words choking in her throat. But with a prayer of thanks in her heart, she cradled her head next to his and wept unashamedly.

Paul licked his dry, cracked lips and cleared his throat. 'What day is it, Beth?' he asked in a raspy voice.

'The first of January. It's New Year's Day.' Just then, Beth noticed a gleam in Paul's eyes.

'A new day, a new beginning,' he responded.

Beth smiled. She was relieved to know that Paul had come through, but wondered just how she would break the news to him about Goldie.

'It's all right, Beth, I know Goldie is dead.'

'But how do you know?'

Paul closed his eyes. 'I just know, Beth. I'll tell you about it later,' and with that, he fell asleep.

Over the following days, as Paul regained his strength, little by little, his story unfolded.

'It was like I was suspended,' Paul recalled. 'From high above, I looked down on the scene. I could see the upturned boat, the moving waves below, and Goldie. I watched as Goldie rescued you from the pounding surf. I saw the stranger on the beach. I saw Goldie return to the ocean. I shouted to him. "It's all right, fella, go back, I'm here. You don't have to go back for me. Leave it. Save yourself."

'But Goldie went on, relentlessly fighting the swell. He plunged beneath the water and, with a surge of extraordinary strength, hauled the limp body to land. It was my body!

'Then I remember looking back at you, Beth. I could see you were worried. I flew closer. "Don't worry about me, Beth," I said. "I'm free, and it's great here." But you couldn't see me, you couldn't hear me, you seemed to look straight through me.

'I turned again and saw Goldie. There he lay, motionless beside my body. I watched. He drew his final breath. At that moment, I felt an almighty infusion of strength and power that I had never experienced before in all my life. A great peace enveloped me. It was then I knew that I would live.'

***

Beth never tired of hearing Paul's story. 'Goldie laid down his life for us, didn't he, Paul?'

'Yes, and I know that he wouldn't have had it any other way. That's real love, Beth. Goldie died so we could live.'

Just then, a soft breeze touched Beth's face. 'Did you feel that, Paul?'

'Yes. Wonder where it came from?'

The two of them sat quietly. Contemplating. Wondering.

Beth's mind went back. She pictured the Labrador standing majestically at the bow of the boat, his front paws on the edge and his face to the wind. 'Do you think that dogs smile?' she asked.

Paul squeezed her hand and gave a cheeky wink. 'Well, I know Old Goldie did, that's for sure.'

Pictures of Last Summer

Helen Iles

Deanna stood looking out across the ocean, the lump in her throat trying to choke the life from her. Waves rolled shoreward in steady succession, tumbling white and frothy onto the sand before their foamy fingers reached outwards to her feet, the expanse of water as profuse as the tears she forcefully held back inside her.

How painful life can be, she thought, struggling to clear the dry patch in her throat and steady her breathing. *How inevitably painful.* But she knew back then it would be. She knew there was no other way out of the developing set of events that had started last summer, events she could have avoided by simply turning and walking away at the beginning.

But she hadn't done that. She'd stayed. She'd felt compelled to stay, and for that she was now being punished.

A tear brimmed on her lid and started its gentle roll down her cheek before she could wipe it away. *No!* she demanded. *Don't cry! You promised yourself faithfully you wouldn't. You came here to relive the good memories, not wallow in the pain.* Indeed, this trip was to regain the good pictures of last summer; she just had to find them.

Swallowing hard, she let her gaze drift down the beach towards the long jetty about a kilometre away. A gentle cross-breeze fanned the waves slightly that way so they met the shore at a tangent, rolling in and stretching flatly against the golden sands where the bay curved further along, then rounded the point at the Yacht Club to the next beach and foreshore beyond.

A dog yapped excitedly well ahead of her, the waves crashing about its feet as it frolicked in the froth before it dashed forward to chase the seagulls off the sand, its liver-red coat rippling and glistening in its flight.

Behind the dog walked a man, a tall, dark, sturdy man, she noted. His trouser legs were rolled up to calf height so he too could enjoy the cooling motion of sea-borne wash. His open-necked shirt and black hair ruffled in the wind, his eyes drawn to the expanse of blue stretching way beyond the line of sight.

Deanna let another glance go his way before turning her attention back to her toes wriggling in the wet, stodgy sand. Something about the man appealed to her. Maybe it was his looks. Even from this distance, to say he was merely handsome was grossly understated. Maybe it was the affection the dog gave to him as it bounded back and forth and leapt about him with a lolling tongue and keen, shining eyes. *Dogs could always be trusted to show good judgment in who they liked*, she assessed, so she knew he was kind, and by the pats he gave the dog, she knew he was lovingly gentle.

I could do with a kind, gentle man. Never again would she take the abuse Ken had wrought on her after their summer meeting. But that was over now. Ken would never touch her again, in any way. She would never let him near her.

The stranger was now much closer, and Deanna thought he looked lonely. His eyes held a void, and his smile was thin as the dog bounded back to him in play, his discontent evident.

She drew her eyes away as he neared her on the beach.

The dog reached her first, its playful bounds around her as it offered itself in play kicking up a stream of sand and splashing. Its tongue lolled from its mouth, gleeful in the glory of its freedom.

Deanna felt compelled to pat it as it loped up to her, its red body rubbing and curling around her in delight as her hands found it, the wetness of its coat transferring to her rolled-up slacks.

'Gyp!' the deep, baritone voice instantly called the dog away, its tone smooth yet dominant. The eyes that chastised the animal were the deepest shade of blue. 'Bad dog!'

'No, it's all right,' Deanna interjected, her jade-green eyes finding difficulty in pulling themselves free from his. 'I like dogs.'

He was almost beside her now, his fingers snapping to call the dog back to his side. 'I'm sorry,' he apologised warmly, his eyes reaching her face for the first time. 'She tends to be a bit boisterous.'

Deanna smiled. 'It's the breed. They never grow out of puppyhood.'

She noted his eyebrow rise at her insight and averted her attention to the dog again. Her hands ruffled its coat as it ignored his finger-snapping command.

'Sounds like you know Red Setters …' He smiled slightly, this time the tightness gone from his lips. She noted his eyes had lost some of that far-off look, too.

She also smiled, warm in the knowledge that, for a moment, his discontent had been eased. 'I have one myself,' she admitted, 'though I stupidly left him behind this trip.'

It was her turn to look slightly forlorn. Sailor would have enjoyed a summer at the beach, a far cry from the small suburban yards of South Perth. She had been too disillusioned to think of anyone but herself when she had packed her bags and headed to Rockingham.

'They do get under your skin, don't they?' the man said with a slightly wider smile.

Deanna nodded but said no more. Her eyes briefly glanced out to sea, an avoidance of admiring the breadth and physique of the stranger standing before her.

Then the Setter bounded off up the beach again, determined to catch at least one of the group of gulls that taunted it just by being there. The man nodded 'Good day' to her and continued to walk after it.

When his back was to her, Deanna's gaze followed him. He might have been that tall, dark stranger on the beach the fortune teller at Stella's party all those years ago had predicted would come into her life … if only she had made a more positive impression. She smiled tightly at the thought. At twenty-five, her luck with men had been worse than dismal. She had been careful to plan her future, her career, her finances, which had all gone rather well; she just hadn't been able to plan much towards her love life. And it wasn't for the trying.

Some days, she felt downright lonely—and would have been if not for Sailor. She decided to send for him. He would enjoy a few weeks of rollicking on the beach rather than being stuck in restrictive kennels.

Then her attention snapped back.

The stranger was walking back towards her.

'I was thinking,' he said, seeming slightly wary about his intentions, 'if you are feeling at a loss without your dog, I wouldn't mind if you wanted to walk Gyp any time. I'm staying at the Seahaven. My work schedule will restrict her exercise, so if you want …'

Deanna knew the Seahaven, a luxury apartment complex overlooking the beach; she had even researched staying there on this visit, but it was beyond her means. She wondered what this man did for a living that enabled him to afford it. Regardless, she immediately liked his offer.

Blinking softly, she looked back at him. 'After seeing you and Gyp,' she said warmly, 'I've decided to send for Sailor to keep me company.'

The man nodded that he understood and turned to walk on.

'But I wouldn't mind exercising Gyp for you,' Deanna added quickly, feeling compelled to do so before it was too late.

The man turned back again, his smile now holding no tightness at all. He looked rather mellow compared to Deanna's first impression.

'The dogs will be good company for each other …' he noted with the hint of a grin. Then his head tilted slightly, and he looked more serious. '… but I've found they are not great conversationalists.'

He looked at Deanna as if assessing what response he would get to his next suggestion, and she smiled at his caution. He seemed a man not fond of failing; he liked to structure his wins carefully.

'Maybe one night, if you feel the need for more interactive company, I could take you to dinner.'

Deanna smiled again – *a gracious host*. Her eyebrow rose pertly. 'Maybe,' she said coyly.

A twinkle lit the man's blue eyes, yet the smile had left his face.

'How about tonight? I'm dining at the Yacht Club.'

Deanna didn't know what to say. This was all so sudden, and the Yacht Club was the most popular restaurant on the resort strip. But she didn't even know his name.

Even so, she was scared she would miss the opportunity to dine with such a gracious man by being so proper and well-planned. Ken had never been so courteous, nor had he shown any insecurities about failing. He just expected.

'I'll be there at seven,' the man added further. 'If you would like to have dinner, just show up. If you don't, I'll see you when you come to walk Gyp.'

Deanna's head filled with what-ifs, as it always did when things threatened her keeping control of her life. What if this? What if that? What if she didn't?

The man looked ready to move on again.

'What if I do?' she asked without commitment.

'Ask for Brent Lanson.' He turned and started walking without even asking her name. The dog raced past him and continued on down the beach.

Deanna stared after him, praying that next year she would not again be sitting here reliving disappointing pictures of last summer.

Rockingham

Dianne Johnson

Do you see God in Rockingham?
His name is printed there.
In God's promises to Abraham
We too can have a share.

Do you see God in RockInghAm?
His name 'I Am' is shown
"I Am" that Great "I Am"
To Moses, God was known.

Do you see God in RocKingham?
See there, the title 'King'
Christ came to earth as God's great plan
To save the world from sin.

Do you see God in Rockingham?
He's there for all to see.
The 'Rock' that o'er the ages span
God's love for you and me.

Rockingham's Embrace

Helen Iles

In the south of Western Australia,
where the blue seas meet the land,
lies Rockingham, a seaside town
where everything is grand.
Glorious beaches stretch like dreams,
kissed by sun and salty air,
families gather on the foreshore,
joy and laughter everywhere.

Dolphins dance on golden waves,
their playful spirits glide,
a ballet of fin and sunlight
as they leap with graceful pride.
Children's laughter rings like bells,
echoes on the warm, soft breeze,
on Palm Beach jetty, fishermen bait their lines,
elusive fish to tease.

The ocean's whisper beckons
swimmers to its gentle, crystal sway,
as sunbeams twinkle on the waves,
and boats moor at the end of day.
Sandcastles adorned with shells and dreams
where, hand-in-hand, lovers wade,
and seagulls swoop and squawk for chips
as the sunlight slowly fades.

Strolling along the vibrant shore,
the foreshore comes alive,
with picnics, games, and sunset hues,
where every heart can thrive.
Here in Rockingham, life's a dance,
a love song of the sea,
where nature's wonders intertwine,
and every soul feels free.

So let the tides embrace your heart,
feel the warmth upon your skin,
in Rockingham's enchanting bay,
where each glorious day begins.
With splendid beaches, laughter's song,
where memories are made each day
this coastal town's a treasure trove,
and why the dolphins come here to play.

Safe Harbour

Christine Draper

I threw a pack of frozen vegetables into my trolley at Woolworths. I was thankful for the cool of the supermarket, as the afternoon was unbearably hot.

'Mum?' asked Lottie.

'Yes, sweetheart,' I replied, trying to calculate how much money I had left for the week. I hated that money was so tight I could no longer afford fresh fruit and vegetables.

'Can we have some oranges this week?'

I bit my lip, running the mental arithmetic. 'Maybe next week, love.'

'But can we please get fish and chips? We haven't had anything from there for ages,' Joel piped up, referring to the popular fish and chip shop on the foreshore.

I sighed, the familiar weight of financial pressure settling on my shoulders. 'Joel, I—'

'Yes, please, yes, please, what Joel said,' Lottie chimed in, bouncing with excitement.

'All right,' I relented, seeing their hopeful faces. 'Fish and chips it is.'

As we approached the cashier, my phone buzzed. A voicemail from Ben, my ex-husband. My stomach tightened. He never called with good news. I tossed it back in my bag, ignoring the call.

After finishing our shopping, we drove to the foreshore and walked to the fish and chip shop. Being a Friday evening, the queue snaked out the door.

Twelve people ahead of us, I counted silently, watching families playing on the park across the road.

'Look, there's Peter!' Joel pointed to his school friend. He'd started at Warnbro Community High School this year, and I was grateful he'd made friends quickly.

'Hello, my name is Lottie. You're a very cute baby,' I heard my daughter say.

I glanced down to see her chatting to a stranger's child. 'Charlotte, what have I said about talking to strangers?'

'But, Mum, look. Isn't she pretty?' I glanced at the child and noticed that she was a child from the daycare where I worked.

'That may be, but her parents didn't come here to talk to a six-year-old.'

'It's okay, she's only being friendly,' her dad said. 'Hi, I'm Jaxon, and this is my daughter Phoebe.'

I looked up. Jaxon had recently enrolled Phoebe at the daycare centre where I worked. Our eyes met briefly before I looked away, the flutter in my stomach reminding me why I'd sworn off men.

'Hi, Jaxon,' I managed.

'Number 302!' someone called out.

'That's us,' Jaxon said, shifting Phoebe on his hip. 'See you Monday, Evelyn.'

'Bye, Phoebe,' Charlotte waved enthusiastically.

As they walked away, Joel asked, 'How do you know him?'

'Phoebe goes to my daycare,' I said.

***

The following week brought changes I never expected. Monday afternoon, I was updating records in the daycare office when Vera knocked. Jaxon stood at the door, his military bearing evident in his straight shoulders and alert eyes. He had told me that he had been in the Navy until last year and now was working in the Kwinana industrial area.

'Evelyn, could we talk?' His tone was more serious than our brief encounter at the fish and chip shop. I felt my heart start to race. I really needed this job ... was he going to make a complaint? Did he think that Phoebe was unsafe here?

'What's wrong?'

'I'd like to speak privately, if that's all right.'

We stepped into my office. 'Is everything okay with Phoebe?'

'Phoebe's fine.' He ran a hand through his dark hair. 'It's about you. I overheard something yesterday, and it concerned me.'

My phone rang. Ben's number flashed on the screen. I let it go to voicemail, remembering I still hadn't listened to his last one.

'Your ex?' Jaxon asked gently.

'Unfortunately.' I tried to keep my voice steady. 'What did you want to discuss?'

'I know it's not my place, but I've been deployed to enough places to recognise when someone's living in fear.'

Heat crept up my neck. 'I appreciate your concern, but ...'

'There are resources available. Support groups. I can help you find—,' he started to say.

'Please, this place is safe.'

'I'm not worried about Phoebe. I'm worried about you.'

'I said I'm fine.' My voice cracked despite my efforts.

Jaxon's expression softened. 'Okay. But I'm here if you need anything. For your children's sake, as well as yours.'

After he left, I sat alone in my office, the weight of his words settling over me like the Rockingham fog that rolled in from the Indian Ocean each evening.

***

The confrontation I'd been dreading came the following

Saturday. Ben's black ute pulled up outside our rental house in Warnbro, the suburb stretching towards the sand hills where we used to take family picnics.

'Where are they?' Ben demanded, his breath reeking of alcohol at ten in the morning.

'It's not your weekend,' I said firmly, blocking the doorway.

'They're my kids, not just yours!'

'Our kids live by a schedule now, Ben. The same one you agreed to.'

His face reddened with rage. I'd seen this progression countless times during our marriage, but now I had to protect myself and the children alone.

'You can't keep me from my own children!' He shoved past me, nearly knocking me down.

'Ben, stop!'

'I'll look for them myself.'

Just as he grabbed my arm, twisting it painfully, a familiar voice cut through the morning air.

'Let her go.' Jaxon stood at the end of my driveway, his presence commanding despite holding Phoebe.

'This is none of your business,' Ben snarled.

'It became my business when you put your hands on her.' Jaxon's military training was evident in his controlled stance.

Ben released me, swearing under his breath. 'You think you're tough. What's it to you?'

'I know I'm concerned.' Jaxon remained calm. 'Evelyn, call the police.'

With shaking hands, I dialled triple zero.

'They'll be here in five minutes,' I announced.

Ben cursed again. 'This isn't over, Evelyn.'

The police arrived as promised, the police vehicle a welcome sight on our quiet Warnbro street. 'What's the situation?'

'Just a family disagreement,' Ben said.

'That's not what I heard,' the police constable said, looking at the red mark on my arm. 'Ma'am, would you like to press charges?'

I hesitated, thinking of my children, their father, the complications.

'She's pressing charges,' Jaxon said firmly.

'That's her decision,' the police constable said, then turned to me. 'Evelyn?'

Jaxon's eyes met mine. I thought of my children watching from inside, of the message I wanted to send them about standing up for oneself.

'Yes,' I whispered, then stronger, 'Yes, I'm pressing charges.'

As Ben was arrested, Jaxon stayed beside me, Phoebe cooing softly. When it was over, he handed me a tissue.

'I'm sorry you had to see that,' I said.

'I'm glad I was here,' he said.

***

Over the following weeks, Jaxon became a quiet constant in our lives. He helped Joel with his homework. He showed Charlotte how to identify shells on Safety Bay beach. Gradually, I let him help me too.

'Why are you doing this?' I asked one evening as we sat on my porch, watching the sunset.

'Because everyone deserves to feel safe,' he said. 'And because I care.'

His words broke something in me. The wall I'd built after a decade of marriage that had taught me to expect the worst started to crumble.

'I'm scared,' I said.

'Of Ben?'

'Of being hurt again.'

Jaxon was quiet for a long moment. 'Fear is understandable. But don't let it stop you from living.'

Gradually, Rockingham began to feel less like a place where I was hiding and more like a place I was healing. The community centre where we now did custody exchanges felt safer than our old arrangements. The daycare continued to be a sanctuary where Phoebe thrived under my care.

But it was Jaxon who helped me rediscover my courage. When Ben's threats escalated, when anonymous notes appeared in my mailbox, when fear tried to paralyse me again, Jaxon was there teaching me that not all men wielded intimidation as a weapon.

Six months after that first confrontation, as we watched our children play in the surf at Point Peron, Jaxon took my hand.

'I love you, Evelyn. Not because I want to save you, but because you're already strong. I just want to be strong with you.'

I looked at our joined hands, at our children laughing in the waves, at this man who had shown me that safety could come with tenderness.

'I love you too,' I said.

As the Indian Ocean stretched endlessly before us, I put my head on his shoulder and realised that for the first time in years, I felt at peace.

In Rockingham, where the land met the sea and the old gave way to the new, I was learning to trust again. One day, one moment, one choice at a time.

Seashore Sunset – Warnbro

Teena Raffa-Mulligan

Warnbro seashore wore
shimmering skirt of shifting hues
in blues and silver
scallop edged with froth of foamy frills.

Dressed in party best
for sunset show
it left me with a
lovely afterglow.

The King of Penguin Island

Dale Kerferd

'Penguin Island, where on earth is Penguin Island?'

'Just south of a holiday village called Rockingham.'

I took a deep breath. 'Deadlines are looming. I don't have time for this.'

My editor placed a tourist map on the desk, pointing to a dot just off the coast, a long way from our offices in Perth.

'I heard that years ago, a British itinerant named Seaforth McKenzie squatted there and called himself the King of Penguin Island. He was probably a nutcase with delusions of grandeur. When the island was gazetted for public use in 1918, the government granted McKenzie a lease, and he developed the island for campers.'

'You know this how?' I paced the room, controlling my impatience with another obscure assignment. 'I will lose a whole day, and how will I get there?' Even in the comfort of the company's latest pride and joy, a Model T Ford, it would take several hours of travel.

My editor, a seasoned journalist with a quirky sense of humour, walked to the window overlooking St George's Terrace. 'I trust my source. Take your camera; the photographer is busy today. The island is also home to a colony of little penguins. It is the only one on the West Coast. It is a pretty area, and you will need pictures for the article.'

He returned to his desk. 'I want it for the weekend magazine, and I am confident you will turn in a winner. Talk to the locals, see what you can find.' He looked at the clock. 'Harry is waiting; he knows the area. I booked the car yesterday, expecting you would welcome a day away from the office.'

'How do I get to this island?' I snapped.'

'By boat. Some bloke runs a ferry service from a shop at the point. There are caves throughout the island, and with luck, some evidence of this strange man's occupancy. Campers still frequent the area, so there must be access from the mainland.'

I was tired and cranky from too many late-night assignments. However, a day in the country appealed to me.

I located the car. Bugger, Ted, might have assigned one of the young drivers to keep me company on that long drive, instead of Harry, who rarely spoke and was not known for his sparkling wit. It was a mystery why he hadn't retired. He opened the back door.

'I'll sit up front with you,' I said, throwing my gear in the back and sitting in the front before he could object.

I read the briefing notes thrust into my hand as I stormed from the office. *Rockingham, 35 miles south of Perth, is a favourite destination for holidaymakers. A former timber port, its reputation for safe beaches and a spectacular coastline attracts people from all walks of life.*

Harry broke his silence as we neared the town, saying it was particularly popular with farmers, eager to enjoy the spectacular summer sunsets and cool breezes. 'And a spot of fishing,' he added.

As fate would have it, Harry and his family had holidayed in Rockingham, and he knew the story about the squatter who lorded it over campers on the island. He said this chap considered himself the King and expected visitors to pay homage. I heard a deep chuckle from my silent companion, and I gathered he found it amusing.

As we approached the town, slowly driving along the nearly deserted beachfront, dark clouds hovered overhead, throwing a midday shadow on the few buildings.

Harry cast his eyes towards the west. 'It has been a wasted journey, I think.'

'How so?'

'A storm is brewing. We might not make it to the island.'

'What do you mean by we? Are you coming too?'

'Of course, Lassie, I know these waters. They can be treacherous, particularly the channel.'

'Humm, storm or no storm, I must file a story, so let's find Penguin Island.'

'It is around the bay. Not much further. The shop should be open for lunch.'

I checked my watch. The sun was overhead, pushing through the dark clouds. 'Food will be most welcome. We have lost the morning, so I assume I will need to gather my information quickly if we are to return before dark.'

My companion nodded. 'Maybe.'

The coastal road scouted around a distant headland, past a few houses, then opened up along the most picturesque bay. Gentle waves lapped the sandy shoreline, and the pristine environment revealed a small island, a short distance from a larger one, I presumed, that was Penguin Island.

I took a breath.

'Beautiful, isn't it, Lassie?'

'Harry, my name is Jade.'

'Yes, Lassie.' His smile smothered my angry retort.

I looked around the bay. Such peace and tranquillity settled my anxiety.

'That is Seal Island.' Harry stopped the car along the beachfront. 'Those black shapes are seals sunning themselves. Not that there is much sun at present,' he chuckled. 'And that is

Penguin Island.' He pointed around the bay to the larger of the two islands.

I opened the door and stepped out of the car. There was a chill in the air, and dark clouds scudded across the horizon, confirming a change in the weather. I dreaded crossing that channel in a small boat. But it was the only way to get my story.

Harry solved my dilemma. 'Mac runs the small store at the point. He is an authority on the island; if he is in a good mood and not too busy, he will answer your questions. Unfortunately, it is too rough to risk a crossing, but he is bound to have a few photographs.'

I swallowed my disappointment. Having come this far, I needed to visit the island. Apart from investigating this so-called 'kingdom', the opportunity to observe the little penguins in their habitat was a rare treat.

'The island is home to several species of bird life, as well as little penguins.' Harry's voice broke my thoughts.

'I am hungry. Let's see if Mac has something tasty besides information.' I opened the door and climbed into the car, determined the day wouldn't be a total waste.

The unsealed road wound around the bay, bringing the island closer as we approached the point. Passing a few beach shacks, the car stopped near a small timber building, nestled in the sandhills.

'Is that Penguin Island?'

He nodded. 'It is only half a mile from the shore. But the crossing can be treacherous. People sometimes walk across, and a few have drowned.'

'It doesn't look very far.' I squinted in the glare from the ocean.

'Take my word for it; it is dangerous if you encounter a crosscurrent. There is a sandbar, and I wouldn't venture out with anyone who couldn't read the conditions.'

I took his word for it. 'Well, let's see if Mac is in today. I am hungry.'

Long plastic strips hung from a narrow doorway facing away from the water. Harry pushed them aside and waited for me to enter. The dark interior of the small shop was unappealing, but pleasant smells emanated from the back. A tall, slim man appeared from the back of the store. He had a full head of hair, a small moustache, and a goatee beard. His appearance was rather ordinary until he spoke.

'Good afternoon,' a well-cultured voice greeted us with a warm smile.

Harry stepped forward. 'It has been a while, Mac. How are you?'

'Harry, my friend, what a pleasant surprise. Who is your charming companion?'

'Good afternoon. I am Jade, a journalist from The West Australian. I hoped to visit the island, but Harry says it is too dangerous to risk the crossing.'

Dark eyes regarded me quietly in what I later recalled as a somewhat aristocratic manner.

'And why would you want to go to the island on a day like this?'

'It was a warm autumn day when we left Perth,' I said. 'My editor wants a piece for the weekend magazine.'

A cool glance passed between the two men.

Harry stepped forward, gently guiding me to a table. 'Let us have lunch, Lassie, then we can weed out the story.'

Mac handed me a menu, and we decided on burgers. Our host nodded and disappeared into the back of the store. The smells were enticing, and I was very hungry.

I turned to Harry. 'What is the problem? I must speak with him if I can't go to the island.'

'I know, Lassie. Give him time. Once we have eaten, he might be more obliging.'

A ray of sunshine pushed through the unwashed windows, drawing my attention to a spectacular view, which settled my anxiety.

'The storm has disappeared.' I turned to Harry. 'We should risk the crossing.'

He shook his head. 'I don't know, Lassie. The weather around here is unreliable.'

Mac reappeared with our order. Plonking them on the plastic-covered table, he asked if we wanted a drink.

'Coffee would be good,' Harry told him.

Mac disappeared again.

'Enjoy your burger, Lassie. I will have a chat with him.'

Despite the shabby surroundings, the burger was one of the best I had tasted. It was undoubtedly a favourite with the locals.

Mac plonked the coffees near our burgers, pushed the plastic strips aside, and walked from the room.

'I hope he returns,' I muttered between mouthfuls.

My companion gave me a rare smile. It transformed his face. I wondered why I hadn't noticed how nice he was. My overactive mind wondered about Harry's age. Maybe he wasn't as old as I thought. Harry finished his burger and followed Mac from the room.

I downed my coffee and followed them outside. The men were standing near the water, examining the sky.

Mac turned as I approached them. 'I think we could make the crossing. Jade, isn't it?'

'Yes. But Harry doesn't think it's safe.'

'Mac is an old hand at this, Lassie. It could be risky, but you won't appreciate the island's character unless you walk among its secrets.'

This could be a good story. 'I am game if you are.'

'It might be bumpy,' Mac warned. 'But I know the channel and all its surprises.'

I looked at Harry. 'Are you coming?

'Of course… Jade.'

I smiled at his use of my name and turned to our host. 'We must return before dark.'

He nodded. 'Follow me. My boat is down there among the coastal dunes.'

'Just a minute.' I raced to the car for my camera bag.

Harry and Mac pulled the small dinghy through the dunes into the water. I skimmed the horizon and noticed the clouds were now a golden glow across the afternoon sky. The storm had indeed passed, but would the crossing be safe?

Mac stood near the boat. I hadn't noticed his high leather boots or the soldier's slouch hat. Standing with his legs apart, hands on his hips, he had an air of authority few would challenge. Mac examined the water separating the island from the mainland. 'Well, come on, in you get.' He placed my camera bag under the wooden seat, then took my arm to assist me into the boat.

Harry removed his shoes and threw them into the boat. He held it steady until I sat, then pushed the boat into the shallow shoreline, hopping in as the small craft splashed and rocked with the current.

My stomach lurched. Never a good sailor, I closed my eyes and prayed we would make it safely across this narrow bay. The men spoke quietly, assessing the channel as they rowed.

Suddenly, there was a loud bump, and water splashed across my shoulders.

'Come on, Lassie, we are there.' Harry helped me to my feet. 'Careful, you need to get your balance.'

For the first time in my life, I was thankful I had worn trousers. Getting in and out of such a vessel was hardly an elegant look. But I had no time for vanity. The day was passing, and I was eager to explore.

The men pushed the dinghy higher onto the sandy shore, safely anchoring it for our return.

'That wasn't too bad, was it, Lassie?'

My head shot up. What happened to Jade? 'No, I guess not.'

'Let me show you around.' Mac took my arm. 'The island is still popular with campers during the summer, though there were fewer visitors this year. I imagine the coming depression has people worried.'

I agreed there were hard times ahead and recalled talk about another war.

Now I had a story to write. 'Where are the little penguins? I would love to get a few photos.'

Mac walked ahead, leading us through the sandy shore onto a hidden pathway towards a tall cliff. He pushed aside the coastal vegetation to reveal a cave buried deep within the limestone walls. I smiled at Harry and followed Mac inside.

The cave was larger than I expected, stabilised with timber and iron struts. A small fireplace and shelves sat under a rocky ledge at the rear.

'This is Manor Hall.' Mac's pride was obvious.

'You have been here before?'

'Oh, yes.'

He led us outside and along the track towards another cave, partially hidden behind the coastal scrub.

'Do these plants have a name?'

'Berry saltbush and wild grape are native to the island.' Harry stooped, snapped a piece of the shrub, and handed it to me. 'You might not see this plant elsewhere.'

I was stunned. 'How do you know?'

'I camped here as a boy.

'Oh!' I had forgotten. Harry had mentioned that.

Mac entered the cave. 'This one is called Tudor Hall. You will notice facilities for campers.'

I spotted tins of canned food on the ground, and books scattered on shelves along the far wall. 'Someone has left a mess.' I focused my camera. The interior was quite dark, and I hoped the flash would capture the essence of the area.

'There was a shop here at one time,' Harry said. He picked up the tins, but left the books. 'It operated on an honour system for campers, and few abused the privilege.'

'The remains of happier times.' Mac looked around the cave. 'I want to show you something, but watch your step.' He took my arm, a rare courtesy these days.

Mac walked ahead, leading us along the track around the limestone cliffs. He pushed aside the foliage along the cliffs to reveal a timber doorway. He shoved it open and stood aside for us to enter.

I lifted my camera, filled with excitement. Did my editor know the importance of this story? What a scoop! The cave revealed a kitchen, a large storeroom, and canvas bedding.

'Did someone live here?'

Mac smiled. 'Yes, he was known as the King of Penguin Island. The locals thought he was a nutcase, but I believe he had more lofty ambitions.'

We followed him from the cave. I needed to discover more about this man. Mac kept on walking, then hesitated. 'Let me show you something of interest.' He brushed away dirt along the track to reveal a stone pathway into another smaller cave. 'This is Fairhaven.' Mac stepped aside for us to enter. It had a musty smell and was much cooler than the other caves.

'It is cooler here.' I looked around and saw a well in the corner and several tables at the rear.

'Campers stored food here from the heat, and that well has water for drinking.'

I was stunned. This far exceeded my expectations, but where were the penguins?

Harry looked at his watch. 'I think we might head back, Lassie. It is getting late.'

'One more thing.' Mac turned and walked from the cave. He waited for us to join him, then continued along the track, taking us further around the cliff. He put his finger to his mouth and pushed aside the vegetation, revealing a small nest. 'It is nearly nesting season, but you might get a few photographs if you are quick.'

Two small penguins raised their heads from the nest, a perfect photo for my story. The vegetation rustled as more small penguins appeared. I felt a hand on my shoulder and turned in wonder.

'It is getting late. The penguins are returning from their fishing trip.' Harry pointed towards the shoreline, where a line of small creatures waddled up the beach towards their nests.

I snapped, consumed by a feverish desire to capture this moment. What a day!

'Thank you.' I took Mac's hand. 'This has been an amazing experience.'

Our host stood, hands on hips, in a very regal pose. He looked at the sky. 'It is time to return to the mainland. That crossing is erratic.'

Mac led the way to the boat. I snapped away, hoping the photos would do justice to my story. On the return journey, I relaxed and held my breath, watching in delight as the sunset lit up the skies behind the island.

I waited for the men to store the boat, then approached our host, shaking his hand. 'Mac, I am so grateful for your hospitality. That was an incredible experience. Did you camp on the island?'

Harry took my arm. 'We must go. It is a long journey to Perth.'

'Ok!' I packed my camera and turned to say farewell. Mac had gone. 'I must say goodbye.'

'No need, Lassie. He knows. Come on, we should leave.'

'Who is he? What is Mac short for?'

Harry opened the car door and waited for me to enter. 'He is Seaforth McKenzie. The King of Penguin Island.'

I was stunned. Harry started the car, chuckling to himself.

The Long Way to Rockingham

Dianne Johnson

Sandra watched the sugar crystals sink slowly beneath the froth of her second cappuccino.

'Still waiting for your sister?' the waitress asked as she placed a plate of toasted raisin bread on the table.

'Yes, and I'm worried. We'd arranged to meet at eleven o'clock and look at the time, it's almost twelve!'

'Don't worry, I'm sure she'll be along soon.'

'But I am worried.' She frowned. 'It's not like her to be late and I've tried her mobile, but it just goes to message.' Sandra took a deep breath and sighed. 'I suppose I'll just have to wait.'

Just then Sandra's phone buzzed. It was Cynthia. She answered quickly.

'Hello. Where are you? I've been waiting for over an hour.'

'Sorry sis, I got delayed by road works and had to detour.'

'Detour! But surely it wouldn't take this long for you to come from Kwinana!'

'Well, the detour took me via Mandurah.'

'Mandurah!'

'Yes, I did a U-turn at the big roundabout, 'cause I know my way back to Rockingham from there.'

Sandra sighed. 'Whereabouts are you now exactly?'

'Rockingham foreshore; I walked past the restaurants, and I've come to the Yacht Club, but I can't see Don't Spill the Beans anywhere.'

'It's not, Don't Spill the Beans.'

'Oh, sorry, Do Spill the Beans.'

'No, it's not Do Spill the Beans, it's just Spill the Beans.'

'Just Spill the Beans,' she tutted. 'I still can't see it.'

'Listen to me. The name of the café is simply Spill the Beans.'

'No wonder I couldn't find it; I was looking for Don't Spill the Beans not Simply Spill the Beans.'

'Never mind about the name.' Sandra said in frustration. 'I'll give you directions. Okay. Now listen carefully. Do you see the jetty in front of the Yacht Club?'

'Yes.'

'Well just a little further south there's another jetty. Can you see it?'

'Yes.'

'Well, the café is directly across the road from that.'

'Just looks like houses and a block of units.'

'The café is situated on the ground level of those units.'

'Oh okay, I'll go get my car and park nearby.'

'Right. I'll see you soon.'

Sandra rolled her eyes. *I can't believe it*, she thought, *who comes from Kwinana to Rockingham via Mandurah! Never mind, at least she's here safe and sound. Well, safe anyway.*

Cynthia parked the car a little way past the café and walked back.

'I really like this,' she said, 'It's very nice. But I'm famished!'

Sandra shifted her bag from off the chair and handed her sister the menu. 'I'll go get you a drink while you decide what you want for lunch.'

'Thanks sis, I'll have an orange juice, please.'

'Right then.'

The sisters enjoyed their lunch together but sadly, because of Cynthia's lateness, their plans to catch a movie were thwarted. Cynthia apologised profusely.

'It's all right,' said Sandra, 'We can do that another time.'

'Why don't we meet in Mandurah next time?'

'What a good idea!' agreed Sandra.

The Love Shack

Lia Eliades

The shack leans
To take in light
It leans from the weight of history
Batten and board
Rub against one another
Peeling paint
Microscopic fibres
Gutters pitted
Rusty holes
Rain washes through
Never making it to the end
Puddling eddy
Swirls at the back door
Threatening to enter time and again
And the kickboard has disappeared
There you can see the layers
Of its life

How many have crossed its threshold
More than it cares to remember
As the boards moaned
And the bed springs
Squeaked
Protesting
Against the
Johns
Who paid
For play and a lay

Local legend has it that 34 George Street, Rockingham, was a house of ill repute frequented by soldiers on leave during World War II.

Treasure Beneath the Waves

Helen Iles

In the balmy days of 2001, the beautiful, sun-drenched seaside town of Rockingham embraced the soft hues of the approaching evening. The gentle shoosh of waves lapping the shore mingled with the soft call of seagulls, creating a serene symphony that settled over the town like a warm blanket.

Daisy Harper had spent most of her life in this coastal haven, filling the pages of her life story with moments of joy, loss, and nostalgia. Today, she had tied her silver hair in a loose bun, slapped the customary tattered sunhat onto her head, and ambled along the sandy beach towards the jetty, gazing at the horizon as the sun melted into the indigo sea.

Daisy's recent days had been filled with the mundane chore of decluttering the house and sheds as she prepared to downsize for a place much less lonely. The task that had shaken her usual routine had, however, stirred her heart. As she crossed over the bitumen slipway a short distance from Palm Beach jetty, she spotted the familiar figure she'd hoped would be there—George Dawson, her long-time childhood friend, who was similarly aged, yet whose years now encumbered him like a tattered coat.

'George!' she called, her voice cracking as it bounced over the wind.

He turned, a smile breaking across his weathered face. 'Daisy! It's been a while.'

'Too long,' she noted, worried now that George would not be capable of achieving her grand intentions.

Nevertheless, their laughter rippled across the water and echoed off the rocks of the Naval Base further along, the sound belonging to a time that seemed both recent and oddly far away. Daisy and George had shared countless summers as children, building castles in the sand and basking in the sunshine of their carefree youth, and as teens and young adults surfing and scuba diving off the islands along the coastline. Now, with wrinkles etched into their skin like they'd been in the water far too long, they had their own stories to tell.

As they settled down on a weathered bench overlooking the water, talk of old times began to flow like a refreshing tide.

'Do you remember that summer in 1931 when we thought we were pirates?' George chuckled, his eyes twinkling with mischief.

'How could I forget?' Daisy replied, a warm chuckle escaping her lips. 'You were convinced we could find buried treasure.'

'Well, technically, I did nearly find some,' he said. 'Don't you remember? The old box your father hid right near the groyne? He ticked us off good and proper for diving near there. Said to leave well enough alone and forbade us to swim there again.'

'And I thought he was pulling our leg, stirring us up,' Daisy recalled, her heart racing at the mention of the long-lost treasure. Her father, a fisherman in his youth, had often spoken in hushed tones about hiding a box of valuables just off Garden Island before the area became part of the naval base—a piece of history now submerged beneath the waves. It was a story that had captured Daisy's imagination, though until recently she'd never thought much of it beyond childhood play. 'Actually, I've been thinking about that box,' Daisy said, her voice suddenly serious. 'I think it's still there.'

'What? Right beneath the Naval Base? George mused, tilting his head.

Daisy's eyes twinkled in the overhead streetlight as she nodded. 'And I am going to go get it.'

George's jaw dropped, exposing aged, worn teeth. 'Isn't that dangerous? Those guards over on the island carry machine guns … loaded machine guns. You wouldn't get within coo-ee of the rocks. They'd shoot your boat to smithereens.'

'Oh, we're not going in by boat, George. I'm not silly enough in my old age to go near the Base above the water. We're going in under the water.'

George's jaw snapped shut again. 'And you said you weren't silly in your old age. And what do you mean … we?'

Daisy turned her head and gave him that look that told him he was going, that look from their youth that told him he had no choice in the matter. Even at eighty, he still shrank back from her whim. 'Daisy, I haven't been diving since that expedition sour when we were sixty.'

'You never forget how to ride a bike, George. It just takes a little practice to get back on the pedals. I've acquired smaller tanks, enough air for us to get the job done without taxing our strength. We can do some practice dives …'

'Do you really think I am going to agree to swimming out to that Base to get shot at by some trigger-happy security patrol so you can attempt to retrieve your father's treasure buried decades ago, which is probably now buried under tons of rocks and rubble where they fortified the island?'

George's back had stiffened with commonsense, raising his courage to stand up to Daisy's proposition. He shook his head firmly.

'What if I said it's not buried under the Base, but under an old mooring 100 metres from the island's point, far enough out they might not see our presence. I found some papers while cleaning out the house, along with a map Dad had made. I am sure this is where he buried his treasure. Just think about it, George. We could fulfil our challenge to retrieve his box of whatever it is.' She sighed pleasantly. 'Oh, I feel like a kid again, George.'

'But you're not, Daisy. Nor am I.'

'Oh, where's your sense of adventure gone, George!'

'I lost it some twenty years back on your last hare-brained scheme. We almost didn't make sixty-one.'

Daisy shook her head and chuckled. Then nodded. Yes, that had been a close call, but she had been planning more thoroughly for this task. And there were no deep-sea helmets or hoses involved this time. Just scuba gear, and they were well-experienced underwater with it.

George continued to shake his head as he looked out at the horizon where the sea met the starlit sky. While his frailty worried her, and probably worried him, she revelled in the fact that he hadn't said an outright No!

***

A determined Daisy and a reluctant George met several times over the next few weeks, training for an adventure they had long since thought lost to time. They completed practice dives around the Palm Beach Jetty and beyond the Yacht Club Marina, George becoming more confident with the lighter tanks and feeling more youthful with each successive dive. Eventually, as Daisy had hoped, he restored his lagging zest for life and embarked on the challenge with an enthusiasm that almost equalled hers.

On that breezy March morning, both stood on the shoreline, scanning the ocean beyond the point of the Naval Base, visualising exactly where the forgotten mooring lay beneath the water.

With the sun low and their spirits high, they piled all their equipment near the boat slips east of Garden Island, a place once filled not with naval presence and armed security forces but childhood dreams. As they donned their lightweight equipment, the silver-haired adventurers were once again children ignited by the allure of hidden treasure.

The tranquil sea called them forth, and they ventured out past the soft lapping shores, their hearts buoyed with dreams and memories. But a heavy air settled around George, both from the chill of the ocean and the weight of apprehension of being shot at. He glanced at Daisy, who stood steadfast, donning her mask after staring at the point with fierce determination.

'I never thought we'd come this far,' he said, breaking the silence.

Daisy smiled, her face a portrait of courage. 'We've come too far to turn back now, George.'

As the sight of the naval base drew their concern, its imposing structure a reminder of the passage of time, they ducked beneath the water and swam a direct line out beyond the pleasure boats moored just off the beach, using them as camouflage, George hampered somewhat by the small shovel they needed to dig under the old concrete mooring slab.

A world of bubbles and sunlight surrounded them as Daisy headed to the ocean floor, her hands groping desperately along the golden sand where shells glistened in the underwater sun, and then …

Daisy's hand scraped along the hard, concrete block, felt the short length of rusted chain lying beneath the silt and sand of the ocean's bed. Looking up, she prayed the surfacing bubbles near the point didn't attract unwanted attention. Surely no one would remember this old mooring that had been deemed out-of-bounds due to being in the exclusion zone around the island. She turned and looked at George, who was also looking up, probably wondering the same thing.

With trembling hands, George began scooping the sand away from around and beneath the mooring, then used the shovel to scoop further beneath it. When a profusion of bubbles escaped from his mouthpiece, Daisy knew he had found something. She joined in the frantic scooping.

With a final grope, she seized and pulled the box from its underwater grave, their breaths coming in gasps, drifting bubbles upward with even more prevalence. For a small box, the weight of it felt monumental, not because it was heavy, but because of the dreams it contained.

Swimming back beyond the moored pleasure craft, retracing their line of entry, they once again reached the shore, slipped off their fins and scurried behind the barrier wall of the slipway, noticing as they did the gathering group of sailors standing on the rocks of the island wall, seriously scanning the water where they had been. They slunk down behind the rocks, examining the package heavily wrapped in layers of waterproof material as they caught their breath. When the sailor group dispersed, they gathered their gear and scurried up the grassy slope to the car, piled it all in, including themselves, the box never leaving Daisy's hand for a second.

Once home, the reveal was as exciting as it would have been in their youth, four hands peeling away the encumbrances that protected the treasure inside. The lock released with an ear-piercing creak.

Inside was a jumble of old-looking coins, bits of jewellery, a journal and a collection of heartfelt letters—love notes between Daisy's parents, she realised, detailing *their* young dreams.

'Oh, look at this!' Daisy exclaimed, holding a delicate silver locket, her eyes shimmering. 'It was Mother's. All these years … I often wondered where it had gone.'

'Your father … he kept them all safe,' George said softly, his voice a warm blanket around her as memories of the early loss of Daisy's mother sank in.

Tears filled Daisy's eyes, not for the loss, but for the love and memories now breathed back into existence.

As the sun dipped below the horizon that evening, painting the sky in glorious shades of orange and pink, Daisy and George shared stories of their youth, their losses, and the joy of reconnecting in their octogenarian years. The treasure, which they had thought would be shimmering jewels, turned out to be something far more precious. It was a treasure of remembrance, a portal to their past, and a catalyst for a friendship that had withstood the test of time.

Daisy, her heart full and buoyed by the day's adventure, felt a renewed sense of purpose. In the gathering twilight, a simple idea flickered in her mind—the old town could use her father's stories, his legacy. So could many children yearning for adventure.

And with George by her side, they started planning to share the treasures they had found—letters turned into tales, dreams woven into workshops for children in Rockingham, and history turned into stories alive with the laughter of children on Rockingham's sandy shores.

With a laugh, George took her hand as they ambled along the foreshore that evening. 'Who knew treasure hunting would lead to this?'

Daisy smiled, her heart lighter than it had been in a long time. 'Some treasures, and houses, are meant to be shared, George.'

And beneath the stars, George held onto the echo of lost dreams and their renewed friendship, and said, 'So, is that our next adventure?'

Walking with Snakes

Sharon X Wong

People will tell you to be careful of snakes in Australia. I mean, they'll also tell you to watch out for spiders, drop-bears, and kick-boxing kangaroos. And it's true that ~~the drop bears do serious harm~~ – I mean, it's true that there are venomous Australian snakes, but to be honest if you live in an urban area you won't see too many. You have to venture into their territory.

Behind Rockingham Hospital, a short walk from my own house, is a nature reserve. My brother and I used to take walks there. It's just about what you'd expect of Australian bush: sandy lanes winding between eucalyptus trees and grass trees. If you go at dusk, you are almost guaranteed to see kangaroos. Go further in and you'll find a salt lake, a water feature completely bereft of any water.

Oh, and you might find snakes.

Image from openclipart.org

When my brother and I first came across a snake, we were young and naive and not very observant. We didn't realise the snake was there until it got stepped on. Or rather, I didn't realise a snake was there until my brother jumped about a foot into the air. My brother's first realisation came when he felt something against his foot, hence the jump. I turned and there was a snake, head reared up from the ground and hissing. Once it ascertained we were more afraid of it than it of us, it slumped back down on the ground. By some miracle, my brother didn't get bitten that day. I'm not entirely sure how, especially as he had donned those most hardy of Australian footwear: thongs. It must have been a near miss.

We saw snakes a few times after that, and having learnt our lesson, stepped on none of them. Usually, they were lying on the path, motionless. At first, we wondered if they were even alive, but then we'd pass it and later return to a snake-free path and know that yep, that had been a living snake we'd stepped over. The first time this happened we did first spend some time semi-cautiously tossing rocks from a distance to see if the snake was alive. Look, we learnt our lesson about stepping on snakes. We had other lessons to learn, obviously. Luckily, our accuracy was terrible.

My brother moved interstate a couple of years ago, and since then, I've been to the reserve many times. However, I have yet to see a snake while walking alone. I'm not sure why. Perhaps I am still not that observant, although I have been keeping an eye out. One thing I have noticed is that someone who lives on the street bordering the nature reserve has a habit of tossing their kitchen scraps on the front lawn in the evening for the kangaroos. This means that you can reliably see kangaroos on that street if you go at the right time – a fact I have taken advantage of when relatives from overseas come to visit. Who needs a zoo when the 'roos are just around the corner?

So maybe the 'roos are distracting me from seeing snakes, or maybe the snakes have found better hiding places. After all, it was my brother who first stepped on one – maybe they don't need to be on the lookout now he's gone. But that doesn't mean I'll drop my vigilance – I've learnt my lesson. When I'm walking in the bush, I'm always on the lookout for snakes. And spiders. And drop bears.

Whispers in the Wind

Mel Young

I can hear whispers
In the wind
Of a time
Long forgotten

Of sunken ships
Bearing the name Rockingham
Of crumbled ruins
That were once dwellings

Of a people who built this place
An old Chesterfield Inn turned dairy
Now boarded up
Who lived there? Who visited?

An old cottage on Day Road
Left to crumble
Really old tombstones
With names of some streets

A ruin once Bell Cottage
A beach front Bell Park
Old abattoir in Hillman
A restored home now office
No admittance
No trespassing
I'd love some photos
Of all these places

Who were these pioneers?
How did they live?
They had a mill
And a quarry

What else did they have?
An inn and a dairy
Farmlands and school
What else, what else?

Why do we not celebrate them?
And learn about them in schools
What did they wear?
What did they eat?

The museum on Kent Street
Has some of their things
But wherever you go, you can hear
Their whispers in the wind.

Contributors

Bernadette Piper

Bernadette grew up in country Western Australia before moving to Perth, where she attended high school.

She worked as an office assistant for many years before backpacking around Europe in the '70s. Returning to Australia, she raised her family and now has three wonderful grandchildren.

Bernadette lives in Secret Harbour and writes from an Australian perspective. She has published *Tomorrow's Roses,* set in Fremantle during 1944-45, and *Tomorrow's Promise*, set in Cottesloe and locations around the world, during the turmoil of the Vietnam War.

Her latest novel, *A Holiday Promise*, which features members of the same family, was released in 2024.

***

Christine Draper

Christine is an author, teacher and mother. She was born and raised in Western Australia; a place she still calls home. She has written over twenty books, from children's picture books to young adult. She is currently writing a paranormal werewolf series.

***

D. Alan Petersen

After arriving in WA in 1988, I had a brief stint in the mining industry before settling down here in Rockingham.

In 2014, three months of long service leave left me with plenty of time to read works longer than articles in motorcycle magazines. Science fiction had been my preferred genre, but the sci-fi of my youth had given way to fantasy, in tomes thick, black and unappealing. What to do?

Answer. The logical thing. Write my own!

A year later, the Rockingham Writers Centre started up. I joined. They helped me develop my writing and broaden my writing horizons.

***

Dale Kerferd

Dale Kerferd joined the Rockingham Writers Group in 2024, after finally returning to her love of writing. She is currently in the final stages of completing her first novel, and has written several short stories, and contributed to several anthologies. Her professional career spanned over 25 years in the newspaper industry, and several in public relations before establishing Sound International Pty Ltd, publishers of RMK Directories. Dale attends the Business of Writing and Aspiring Writers workshops.

***

Danny Whitehead

Danny Whitehead's love of words and writing led him to seek a career as a librarian in the local libraries of Rockingham. Working amongst some of the great titles in the literary world fueled his passion for writing. With two-thirds of his first novel nearly complete, Danny turned to the Rockingham Writers Centre for help. Attending the Emerging Authors group on a Thursday night has boosted his confidence to finish his novel.

***

Dianne Johnson

Born in Sydney NSW, Dianne now resides in Perth, Western Australia with her husband Jim. They have six children, nineteen grandchildren and eight great-grandchildren.

Dianne's desire to write was evident from a young age – long before she could either read or write! She writes poems, skits and short stories and has won awards in two National Literary Competitions. Her published works include:

A novel, *In Search of Love*, her memoir, *Fragrance of Life*, a children's picture book, *Ben and the Muddled-up Moon*, together with poems and short stories in several anthologies.

***

Georgia Tingley

Georgia Tingley began her career with her first novel *Justice*. Now, with six books and a handful of awards to her credit, she has never looked back. Having lived in various countries while growing up – India, England, Canada, and New Zealand – she now calls Western Australia home. Living near some of the best beaches in Australia, she loves to swim, snorkel and ride her bike along the foreshore. In her downtime, she loves to read, watch movies, do crafts, and get into the garden. She and her husband enjoy taking the caravan on trips into the Australian Outback and seeing as much of the 'red country' as they can.

***

Helen Iles

Helen Iles is a novelist, poet, lyricist, children's author/illustrator, editor and publisher. She is a creative writing coach, Chairperson of the Society of Women Writers WA, and a committee member of the Rockingham Writers Centre.

She opened Linellen Press in 2000 with the aim of assisting West Australian authors achieve their dream of being published.

Her titles include *Bitter Comes the Storm, Fire in the Heartland, The Horse Keepers, Dark Secrets,* and numerous children's picture books, most recently *Cuddles with Prickles*. CD albums *Lyrical Dream, These Country Boots,* and *The Gravity of Us* showcase her song lyrics which are available on Spotify.

***

Jean Frost

With her love for all things Horror and Fantasy, Jean Frost was awarded a High Commendation in the Coral Coast Short Story competition. Jean has served on the committee of the Rockingham Writers Centre as Writers Coordinator for the last four years, moving up into the role as Chairperson of FoRAC last year. She is published in several anthologies, including those of the Warnbro Writers, Serenity Press, and Rockingham Writers Centre.

***

Karlene Jolliffe

Karlene Jolliffe is a writer of poetry and short stories. Painfully shy as a child, her happy place was anywhere alone where she could read, write, draw and imagine. Spending so much time in made-up worlds, unsurprisingly, her most favourite and best school subject was creative writing. As life progressed, story writing fell by the wayside in favour of other creative pursuits, but her love of words saw her formally study the craft in her late thirties. Two decades on, Karlene now writes across a range of genres, and her work has been published in local and national anthologies.

***

Kathy Flint

Kathy Flint was born in England and migrated to Perth with her family as a teenager. Kathy previously worked for over thirty years with the Federal Government, writing Human Resource policy and articles which were published on the intranet. In 2001, her work was recognised when she received an Australia Day Award.

Now Kathy is retired and writes happy, uplifting stories just for the joy of it. Kathy has recently published a collection of short fiction, *Searching for Perfect*, about everyday people searching for their idea of perfect. She is currently working on her first novel.

***

Lia Eliades

A creative spirit from New York City's Lower East Side, Lia has lived and worked across Thailand, Indonesia, China, and now Western Australia. For the past 28 years, she has balanced life between a broadacre farm on the edge of the Outback and the shores of Rockingham. Her writing spans poetry, short stories, and a debut novel currently in progress. Lia's work has appeared in online literary journals, the *WA Poets Anthology*, *Poetry d'Amour*, and various writing group collections, reflecting a deep engagement with place, memory, and the stories that connect people across landscapes.

***

Mel Young

Mel Young grew up by the ocean in Western Australia, with a passion for history and fantasy. Forever the storyteller, she has penned short stories and poems throughout her life. In 2018, one of her stories and a poem were featured in an anthology produced by the Rockingham Writers Centre as part of a mental health project, Out of the Blue. Mel hopes to one day publish the novel she has been working on for the past year.

***

Nada Lubay

Nada Lubay embarked on her writing journey at the age of 60, motivated by her granddaughter. Despite English being her second language, she pursued her dream of becoming a writer and joined the Rockingham Writers Group and the Society of Women Writers WA, consistently attending writing classes to improve her skills. After years of perseverance and learning, her debut novel, *The Silent Heroines*, was published in 2022.

In 2024, she released her second book, *Tears of an Angel*. She is now working on a collection of short stories, and a new novel, *Belly Dancing Princess*, for a 2026 release.

***

Rosanne Dingli

Rosanne Dingli has published short and long fiction, winning several accolades, since 1990. She has held a number of salaried editorial positions and has lectured in Creative Writing. Her fifteen novels, six novellas and several collections of short fiction centre around the classical arts, such as painting, music, and literature. She also uses history, and locations and their allure, to anchor her stories in reality and give them substance.

**

Sharon X Wong

Sharon lives in Rockingham, Western Australia, but spends most of her time in completely imaginary worlds. When not earning money wrangling documents and figures, she writes stories in many flavours of speculative fiction. She enjoys rambling podcasts, symphonic music, and walks in the park.

**

Sue Sacchero

Safety Bay author Sue Sacchero's Great War novel, *Valiant Hearts* was published in April 2025.

Descended from First Fleeters and Irish Rebels, Sue is the seventh generation of her family to call Australia home, and has a lifelong interest in Australian history, particularly colonial history.

Sue is a member of the Swan Chapter of the Fellowship of First Fleeters and a volunteer curator at the Army Museum of Western Australia.

Sue likes to stay physically fit. She walks and swims most days and practises yoga. In June 2025, she completed the 2000-kilometre walk from Canterbury Cathedral to the Vatican.

***

Teena Raffa-Mulligan

Teena Raffa-Mulligan writes quirky and whimsical children's books, fun, flirty romances and contemporary women's fiction. She is the author of more than 20 books full of heart, gentle humour and hope for young readers, and her short fiction and poetry for children and adults has appeared in anthologies and magazines. Teena is passionate about the importance of storytelling in our lives and enjoys inspiring people of all ages to set out on their own story adventure.

***